THE
ENDO PROJECT

Humanity. Technology. Daihumanism.

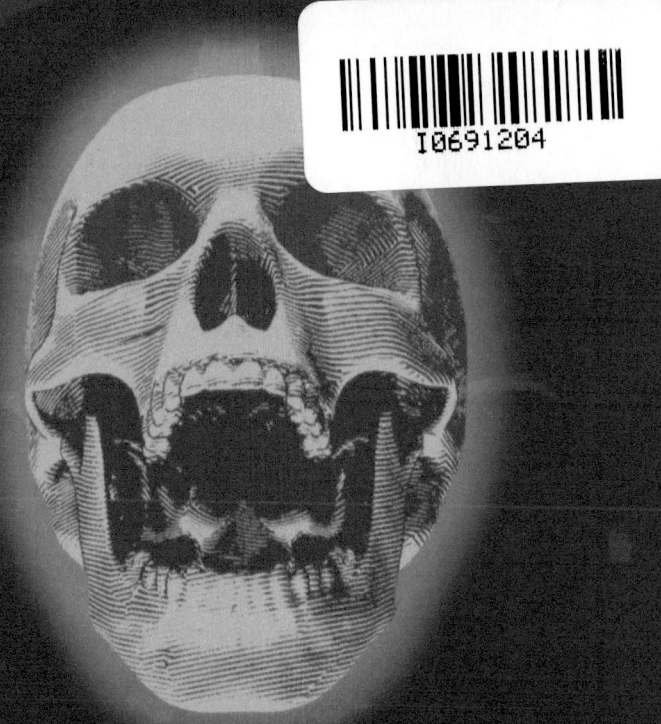

Paperback ISBN: 979-8-9909051-0-8

Library of Congress Control Number will be given upon request.

Front cover art used under license from Shutterstock.com

Front Cover Art done by Angela Moore.

Printed in the United States of America.

First edition printing.

Art within the book is created by Awangga, Kawateo, Nuwan Tharaka Sarathchandra, and Doan Trang.

Publisher information
RaeKLPublishing@outlook.com

www.theendoproject.com

Table of Contents:

1… page 7

2… page 10

3… page 13

4… page 19

5… page 23

6… page 27

7… page 33

8… page 36

9… page 40

10… page 44

11… page 48

12… page 53

13… page 60

14… page 63

15… page 68

16… page 73

17… page 78

18… page 84

19… page 89

20… page 97

21… page 103

22… page 111

23… page 115

24… page 122

25… page 128

26… page 134

27… page 145

28… page 163

29… page 168

30… page 176

31… page 182

32… page 188

33… page 196

34… page 213

35… page 222

36… page 227

37… page 232

38… page 236

39… page 240

40… page 242

41… page 253

42… page 270

43… page 277

44… page 289

45… page 291

46… page 293

Credits… page 295

About the Author… 296

Whatever it takes, be kind to yourself.

14,572

To all of my fellow American people. It is hard to understate the tragedies we've been facing. Overpopulation, famine, climate change, lack of employment opportunities, unaffordable housing, the spread of contagions—among many other factors.

We've been struggling for the past decade. Some far more than others. Keeping our families fed in the midst of the overpopulation crisis has left a lot of us stressed, and resentful towards the institution who is meant to support them.

During my presidency, my team and I have passed or reevaluated numerous legislation to try to alleviate the aforementioned problems. These issues previously mentioned are not a difficulty only in America, but the entire world. No single country has been able to escape these struggles or come up with a permanent solution that helps soften the challenges which humanity has been thrust into.

That to say, it has been rumored for quite some time and I am here to officially confirm it. The End of Life bill has reached the Congress floor and will certainly be implemented into official American policy.

All Americans that are of eighty years of age or older will have the opportunity to participate in willful euthanasia. This will be painless; you'll be surrounded by your family, and your method of preferred burial will be guaranteed and paid for by the government. Along with these conditions, the family of the participant will receive fifty thousand dollars to do with what they wish.

This money will be received in installments and is nontaxable. There are also other programs currently in development to support the beneficiaries to which family members have participated.

The money received by the beneficiaries can be reinvested, used to purchase necessities such as utilities, food, and rent or mortgage. The money can also be housed in a retirement fund, whose value increases every year. If the next member of your family chooses to participate in this End of Life program the yearly rate will increase further, and even more if another family member participates.

Think of this as a dedication to not only your country, but the future of your family and your community's growth. Participants in the End of Life program will have exactly one month to decide on willful euthanasia or all the program's money will be forfeited.

This program is not mandatory. Any elderly found deceased not through a registered government facility will have all funds from the program revoked for that victim's family. Legal action will be taken against those suspected of foul play, and in the future the alleged perpetrator or convicted family will not be eligible for funding through the program.

The End of Life program is an absolute last resort for not only our nation but the entire world itself. If proven to be a failure, new programs will be developed to combat the current economic and environmental issues, and the End of Life program will ultimately be withdrawn.

As an elder of eighty-one years of age, I intend to participate in this program the moment my presidency ends. This is to continue serving my country, and if my presidency were to end by morning's light, I would not draw breath overmorrow.

Not only do I feel this is my duty as an American, but it's the only option I see for any hope of escaping the never-ending struggle to survive in this world we have created.

For further questions please contact your local government agencies. Thank you and God bless you all.

165

Hello, my name is Cassandra Moore. I used to be a cybersecurity specialist for BeyondBio. For those unaware, they were a biotech company specializing in cures for manmade pathogens and also—although it was much less of their focus—an AIHA[1] distributor and installer.

Long ago, I decided to document the feelings and opinions of the world's citizens, especially the American people whom I've lived among my entire life. Interviewees include those involved in legislation as well as those affected by said legislation.

I have no idea why I started this endeavor. Perhaps it was simple curiosity. Then it sort of spiraled into this obsession of interviewing people from around the world. But, if people ask: I'm a true-blooded America patriot and I have an overwhelming fascination with our countries pre and post Reset history.

While digging deep into the programs that were passed over the years before, during, and after Mr. Wile's presidency, I have discovered many interesting things I would like to share with you all. These interviews are from anywhere between the years 2042-2080. You'll be greeted by a *much* younger Cassandra, who was the one conducting these interviews. This is my own personal submission to the End of Life program's participant website.

Firstly, I'll be including snippets of the best and most interesting interviews I've acquired over my numerous

---

[1] *Artificial Intelligence Home Assistant*

years of traveling the world and America. These will tackle topics such as "The End of Life Program", "The Misinformation Age", "The Great Reset", and "After the Reset".

Next, I'll include my own personal story, at least what I find worth telling, or what someone on this platform might find compelling. This is customary for submissions to the End of Life program website.

Lastly, I'll include some of the discoveries and recordings I had while in "THE TRENCH" or "The Lost Web" as a former "DIE.VER", near the end. Don't worry. I'll include the far more interesting bits that are not about myself here in the beginning. These interviews I believe to be the absolute best culmination of my life's work.

Although, there is one final part after everything else. Even if none of this submission sticks with you, please pay attention to the final part: Daihumanism. It's a concept that I hope is not ignored or forgotten.

Carefully consider the order in which I've placed the content here for you today, and why I have chosen this order. These interviews are intentionally placed out of order and the dates on which they were recorded isn't listed. Thank you for taking your time to be here with me today. Please enjoy.

Part 1: The End of Life Program

> *This interview is conducted with Brenda De Lacy, her claim to fame being that she's a former secretary of President Wile, often considered the greatest U.S. President to have ever lived. This interview is occurring thirty-five years after Wile's Assassination.*

How do *I* feel about the Endo program, Cassandra? Well. I think it's abhorrent and you wouldn't catch me dead participating in that rotten program.

Brenda takes a hit on her vape and expels the fruity flavored vapor.

Although, when I think about it, I think Wile would've been okay with it. He was always trying his best for the people, although I don't think he would've come up with this "solution" on his own.

"You mentioned Wile. Considering you worked closely with him, do you have any thoughts on his presidency?" I asked.

Close with him? *Heh*. Whoever told you that? I met him a couple of times, I just helped him communicate with his opponents. Building common ground and stronger relationships behind the scenes. Not as difficult as you might think. Mostly it's just communication. People just don't want to talk with those whom they consider their opponents. You have to convince them that what they want isn't what they're doing currently or that you're ultimately on the same side. People were entrenched in a very old belief system when I was serving with Wile. He was the most dedicated man I had ever met, working around the clock. He went gray within his first year. I don't know if he ever slept. Wile had to be a robot.

"You mentioned working with his opponents. What was it like being a part of politics during the most transformative years in American history?" I asked.

It wasn't as exciting as it seems, in hindsight. The bureaucracy during Wile's presidency was legendary, we have yet to see something even half as competent. Passing free and reduced healthcare in the pharmaceutical giant dominated industry is nothing short of a miracle. When you include everything else he has done? By far the best president to have ever lived.

Name a *single* president that brought both the left *and* the right together. Wile knew how to talk to people. Understand people. He actually really cared about the development of this country. Taking on the former corporate America must have been dangerous, obviously.

Brenda takes a large puff of her vape and is silent for a moment before expelling the vapor.

Actually, let me change my answer from earlier. Now that I say all that, I don't think Wile would've dreamed of the Endo program. Do you think a single human life is worth fifty-thousand dollars? Sure, it's a good replacement for hospice care, but it's just the *idea* of it that bothers me. Legally killing yourself and incentivizing people to do it? Something shady is going on behind the scenes. That much I am sure of.

In all of my years working in politics, never would I or anyone in my cabinet ever have thought Endo was a good idea. I would rather kill myself than participate in something like that. You hear how people's families try to coax their own parents into participating? Trying to manipulate some of our most needy members of society?

Brenda takes another hit of her vape.

Ridiculous. If my kids *ever* come to me with these Endo shenanigans...? I think I might actually kill them.

"Kids? Tell me about them," I asked, waving my hand in front of my face.

I have three children; all are somewhat successful. Tommy was interested in business until he wasn't, he's studying to become a doctor now. He cares more about people than financial stability. I told him it wasn't very wise. We haven't spoken since.

The pay just isn't worth the effort, in my opinion. I mean, they did make it easier to become a doctor now, probably because of the lack of interest in the field. The other two are off in some country like China, looking for different economic opportunities.

"Do you think the End of Life program has improved your life since its inception?" I asked.

Improved how? I have seen the statistics, who hasn't? Play them on the news every other week, it feels like. They are so clearly cherry-picking evidence to make the program look more beneficial than it really is.

Think about it for two seconds. We have a vast homeless population, most of which are old and starving. What a fancy coincidence that most of our homeless were well over the minimum age required to participate in the Endo. Our elders were completely and totally neglected by the government who was supposed to help them. Not to mention, it wasn't their fault they lost their homes, but we're all very familiar with that concept. Then, one day, out of seemingly nowhere, "Hey, you can get your demented, crack addicted grandma to kill herself so you can buy one of our GBHs[2]?"

Most of that fifty-thousand dollars went right back to the government just so people could've had half a decent life. They weren't going to do a goddamn thing about the homeless epidemic, and we all knew it.

Yet another exhale of cherry plum flavored vapor.

And if I may add, if Wile didn't extend Section Eight benefits for those outside the poverty line and to combat the absolutely avaricious housing market, everything would've failed. The Endo, education developments, technological replacement—everything. Without Wile, the Endo would've been another worthless attempt at fixing the issues perpetuated by the older generations who "kicked the can", so to speak. Wile was crucial in the success of the Endo. Without him it would be as

---

[2] *Government Built Home*

worthless as every president after Wile himself, including Berkley. I'm glad he's dead. Despite my comments, the Endo should be illegal. I can't believe I supported a government who made such an autocratic decision.

"You seem to feel strongly about the End of Life program," I said.

I do. This whole situation is ripe with conspiracy. Everything worked out *too* well. With less people who are inactive in the growth of our economy; of course, GDP, food insecurity, homelessness percentage and things of that nature will look as if they're improving. Homelessness has gone down because the homeless elders killed themselves for their family, and then their benefactor is buying an—albeit affordable—house at a discount whose funds go directly back to the government. It's genius, I'll give them that. And how did they convince the homeless to abandon their lifestyle? I thought most of society had given up or was addicted to drugs. Those types of people aren't exactly known for giving that life up on a whim.

"For those tired of wandering, it seems to have worked out that way. But also, it had a lot to do with alleviating symptoms of addiction, I believe," I said.

That isn't enough to just convince people like that, trust me. We tried. There are more factors you and I are not aware of. Do you really think that every single study only has positive affirmations to say about Endo? I wouldn't be surprised if something came out that there was a gag order on all documentation that makes the program look bad in any way.

Makes sense too. That isn't even half as corrupt as some of the things I saw first-hand, and that are probably still going on now. But people aren't malevolent, they just want to protect themselves and their investments. Some just go about it in ways that are more... self-serving.

Brenda takes another puff of her vape.

On top of everything else, the government also monitors your spending with that money. Can't be transferred out of the bank account they give you for it. Only goes to reputable sources or retailers approved beforehand. Total control, absolute fascism. I don't know, Cassandra. Seems Machiavellian to me. People die for that money, why not let their family do what they want with it?

This interview is with Kyle Hart, a self-proclaimed member of what used to be known as the Republican Party. Kyle lives with his family in a GBH in Whitewater, Wisconsin. The home is what you would expect from a first generation GBH. Popcorn ceilings, off-white walls, and uninspired architecture.

Hmmm. Well, it's interesting, that much is true. I ain't really thought of doin' it myself, but I know my father did. Really helped me out of a bind. I used to think it was kind of medieval, but when my dad came to me 'bout it, all I could think was, "Well, it ain't really my decision." He must've been one of the first people to do it.

I don't really think of it as killin' yourself neither. Like, the places are beautiful, for one. Where you do it, the uh… procedure. Real quick and easy. They also asked me tons of questions before my dad could even participate, since I was the sole member of his family that was gonna be gettin' the money.

I think I tried to ask him for a week, but he had already been in pain since early 2040. Had a real bad accident at work, I told him not to be workin' but he ain't listen. Gone and messed up his spine, had to put these plates in it. Said he could tell when a storm was comin' just from the sting he'd get in his ass. Suffered for a decade, that is until the Endo program was made.

Had to move from Florida where we lived after his accident. They had been building homes that were pretty decent. Tried to reduce 'mount people had to drive in areas. I don't remember the last time I actually drove a car. Sold my truck to some collector of gas-powered vehicles couple years back. I was able to pay off this home from the truck and the money from the Endo.

"What do you have to say to the critics of the End of Life program?" I asked.

I can see it from their point of view. Ain't really a natural thing to do, if you ask me. If my dad wasn't so adamant 'bout doin' it, I would've pushed back a little more. But I think we're much better off now, and people ain't think of it like that.

Yeeeeeeeep. They see it as theys people killin' themselves for fifty big ones. It ain't like that at all. My dad was in pain every day, we wasn't homeless, but we may as well been. They ain't give out pain meds like they used to. Even when most of everythin' free, you had to basically be dyin' to get some painkiller.

He had a real bad drug addiction 'cause of it. It's 'cause of "cooperative livin'". Dealers everywhere, people traded drugs like candy for services back in the day. I ain't so proud to admit but I got my dad some fentanyl a couple times, so he wouldn't be in pain. Broke my god damn heart. But I couldn't let him suffer, ya know? Every decision I made felt like it was the wrong one. But better to feel nothin' then be livin' in pain.

"I'm sorry you had to experience that, Kyle," I said, mournfully.

It's fine, Cassandra. But that's how people were livin' back then. Privacy was deader than roadkill. An outhouse would've been an improvement to those livin' situations. Hell, I remember a time where you couldn't walk down the street without seein' trash or someone sleepin' in boxes or on a ragged piece of tarp or somethin'. It got to the point where so many people were beggin', ain't no one really beg no more. Too much competition.

Worst of all, let's not forget that one guy who went out to kill them homeless people for fun. It felt as if no one was safe. Say what you want 'bout the program. But it saved me from a life that wasn't much worth livin'.

"You said before we started that you were a member of the former Republican Party; how do you feel about the removal of our former parties labeling in politics?" I asked.

At first, I thought it was crazy. Take away the American people's identity? That don't sound like freedom to me. How was I supposed to know who to vote fer now? Lot of controversial stuff happened when Wile was around. Probably thought he was genius for removin' the party labels.

Yeeeeeeeep. Didn't do much of anythin' either. People just started callin' themselves somethin' else. But then I had to look at what these parties represented, and I ain't like what I seen.

They were clearly just tryin' to manipulate us. Like, The Free Thinkers Party, what does that even mean? Really made me avoid those people like the plague. I started to pay attention to what they was sayin' now, instead of votin' for the same party every time like my dad did. Wile really turned our whole government on its head, I'll tell you what.

That's why I call myself a former Republican now, reminds people that what you got ain't so bad. It used to be a lot worse.

This interview is with Eren Stein. A researcher of Endo depression from Germany, the second country in the world to adopt the End of Life program, after America. He'll give me his perspective on why he thinks the German government was so quick to adopt the End of Life program, even when he believes it wasn't necessary for Germany at the time.

I think the Endo program is an interesting idea, to say the bare minimum on it. Our government wasn't necessarily struggling, but they weren't thriving either. Germany adopted the program for those sixty-five years or older, but there were no time restraints with participation.

An interesting twist on the time-sensitive American version of the program, but it works. It gives those peace of mind towards the end of their life that their burial will be covered. Their family is also not going to have to worry about finances as much after they're gone. Sort of like a guaranteed life insurance policy for German citizens. Although, the follow up on the reduction of policies meant to benefit those sixty-five years or older isn't a coincidence, I fear.

"That seems to be a common factor all over the world," I said.

It's only natural for the young to benefit the young. After implementation of the Endo, food became plentiful again. Germany in 2051 had an elder population of about forty percent. Now that number has dropped to a little over twenty-three percent. This is a vast improvement. The economy is much more active, and we have partnered with other countries to help them succeed when implementing the End of Life program, or as we call it, Letzte Getränk[3].

"Interesting. But didn't you say that it was weird for Germany to adopt the program so quickly?" I asked.

It was. At the time, it had only been four months since the U.S. adopted the program. There was no data to support whether it was a good idea or not. No studies confirming its effectiveness, just ridicule for the insanity of that which the U.S. was committing. But out of nowhere our government announces a similar program! The citizens were furious to say the least, and I was too.

But then our citizens started to use the program on their deathbed, got their money, and had their funeral expenses covered. Truly a remarkable turnover for those who were already on their way out.

"And Germany is better off now?" I asked.

I would say so, it was just so suspicious that we adopted it so quickly. It made no sense. Our government was steady, we managed to stay out of the "Water Wars", back then. Our allies were all working together. We had one of the happiest populations on Earth, and then our chancellor announced their version of the Endo.

It was like if you were getting perfect marks in secondary, and then your parents reprimand you for not taking out the trash once.

---

[3] "Last Drink"

"Harsh" is the first word that comes to mind. At the time I was a student in university, obtaining my master's in psychology. But when this program came out, I was interested in doing some studies about its nature and the development of those who wanted to participate.

"That's when you started to notice some weird behaviors?" I asked.

Yes. It took about four years, but those who anticipated participating in the program were much, much unhappier than everyone else. If they set up an appointment for, let's say... three years down the road. Every year we measured how patients were feeling mentally. A consistency appeared. Not a single patient reported feeling an overall increase in happiness as we did our yearly evaluations. The patients would say they were consistently feeling much more anxious and careless in their own actions. This anxiety and stress would increase as the end date approached.

Then we started measuring their brain activity. All of the "happy chemicals" were down. Those willing to "sacrifice" themselves were suffering. They commented that their family relationships were degrading. And at this time, I actually read your book *The Endo Project*, and I was truly inspired.

"Thank you," I said.

Yes. It was brilliant. I then dubbed the phenomenon "Endo depression" partly to acknowledge your incredible work, and to call it what it was.

Our elders were sacrificing not only their lives, but their quality of life. Those who preemptively committed to making an appointment were most affected by Endo depression. We now know the looming societal expectation is enough to degrade the quality of an elderly individual's life. Some patients started showing symptoms of Endo depression as early as three years before the expected date of participation, but, as research develops, that number may change.

Developing any type of illness also increased this anxiety further. Every metric of happiness, family stability, family relationships and friendships all went down for elders who were participating in the Endo. It is very important to me that we do something about this.

Currently, we are working on new medication to help alleviate these symptoms of unhappiness. We are hoping that we can help the transition to End of Life care be a smoother process for individuals that are willing to participate in Endo. We hope to see success with our research in the next five years, but it could take longer.

Dr. Redmond is a neurosurgeon at the Orlando Health Regional Institute. He's a doctor pre and post End of Life program, he has even seen the days when medical technology was dominated by robotic surgeons. The nature of the interview will talk about the End of Life program and the current state of the medical complex post End of Life program in Dr. Redmond's opinion.

Do you hear me okay?

"Yes," I said.

Perfect. What would you like to talk about first, Cassandra?

"I would like to know your thoughts on the End of Life program," I said.

Sure! As a Doctor, I know we take the Hippocratic Oath. "Prescribe the most beneficial treatment" and "try your best to not harm the patient further from our treatment", in layman's terms. But in my opinion, that isn't always best for the patient. I have been saying this for years. Humans became too obsessed with saving lives. Sometimes, letting a patient pass on is the best way to treat them.

We don't live in a magical society, hell, the medical industry is still trying to train competent doctors after The Great Reset. Luckily for my hospital, they had a few older surgeons, including myself, who were trained and running simulations to maintain a level of competency when it came to surgeries.

But back to what I was saying, the End of Life program has been a miracle for a majority of my patients that have been suffering. Pre-End of Life program, you stick it out, try a different medication. When that medication inevitably failed you? Try another medication. When *that* medication failed as well? Try another. This was an endless loop I saw all too often. People think since the medical industry was so advanced back then, that we had a cure for everything. We didn't. In my opinion, we have even fewer cures now.

Dr. *Redmond clears his throat.*

Do you know how to make penicillin, off the top of your head? What about Excedrin? Midol? Simple drugs prescribed every day. Gone. Now what about doxorubicin or cladribine? We lost all of that knowledge with The Great Reset, and cancer is such an incredibly destructive disease, and it has no single solution. We have treatments, plans, methods, and some have worked, but not all do. And... are you okay? You look dizzy.

"Yes, I'm fine. Just, um... keep going." I cleared my throat. "Please continue."

Apologies. All of that to say. This was a way out for people who were suffering. Instead of dying for nothing, you could at least get some sort of monetary value from your death. Funerals are expensive, know what it costs to die naturally? More than most can afford. I would only recommend the End of Life program to those who were only living to continue an existence filled with pain. I think the idea of the program is dystopian, but it has helped out hundreds of people so far. Only more will benefit from this program in the future.

"Interesting insights, doctor. Let's change topic. Why do you think nanomachines never made a comeback?" I asked.

When healthcare became free, nanomachines were a lot less interesting to investors. They were around, yes. But they never really made it out of the trial stages when the Reset happened. It was just far easier for an AI to treat and prescribe medicine to patients and do the surgeries. We see now how that became such a problem.

"You just said investors lost interest in the medical field. Would you like to elaborate on the current state of the medical field and why people and investors may feel that way?" I asked.

I hate this question, no offence.

"None taken," I said, casually.

Before, certain individuals were just becoming doctors or getting into the medical field because it was profitable for themselves. Once healthcare became free and the industry became a lot less lucrative, of course a lot of "doctors" would switch industries. They were just there to turn a profit from suffering.

They didn't care about the patients or their treatment, they only cared about the unreasonable amount of cash that the industry they had chosen was raking in.

You know what we have now? Every single doctor, RN, med student, pharmacist, LPN and tech that I meet is enthusiastic about helping people.

Patients understand this too. Sure, everyone is making a little less money. Sure, it isn't as easy to get seen by a doctor. But now people have peace of mind. They don't have to wonder if they can afford their treatment anymore.

Know why hospital waiting rooms are at capacity so often? Because people don't sit and ignore that looming pain they've had for three weeks nipping away at their abdomen. They come to the doctor's office. They seek the help they need. If that doesn't convince people that it was for the best, I don't know what will.

Dr. Redmond clears his throat, again.

Know how many times I had a fellow "doctor" prescribe aspirin to a patient who had a brain bleed just because they were complaining about a headache? An absolutely insufferable amount.

What I'm saying is, nothing is ever perfect. In a perfect world we wouldn't have had ten point five billion people nearly starving. In a perfect world no one would get sick. In a perfect world we wouldn't have suffering. But we don't live in a perfect world. The "End-o—"

Dr. Redmond coughs loudly into the microphone.

"Endo?" I asked.

Sorry, choked on my water, The End of Life program.

"I think that had a nice ring to it, doctor, 'The Endo Project'. Don't you think? 'Endo' for short?" I asked.

Sounds fine, rolls off the tongue better. The official name is a bit of a mouthful.

"I'm sorry. Thank you, doctor. We can continue the interview."

Part 2: The Misinformation Age

This is an official news broadcast by the BBC. I recovered this broadcast from The Lost Web. This announcement has not been seen since its original broadcast.

Today's top story:

A terrorist organization allegedly working with Witnesses of Singularity have claimed to be spreading a deadly contagion in the London Underground, and that thousands may be infected.

As our viewers, you're advised to stay indoors and not have any contact with anyone who has been outside in the past two weeks. For more information on this situation as it develops, check the government notification sent out to your cellular device or neurochip.

All flights to London for the foreseeable future have been canceled and the Prime Minister is calling for a nationwide lockdown outside of London. We are going to play the video sent in by the terrorist organization now.

A man—suspected to be an AI generation—stands in a room with flickering lights, and has the same voice as the King of the United Kingdom at the time of this broadcast.

"The time is now, citizens. The end is nigh. At twelve p.m. over two weeks ago, we sprayed an odorless, tasteless, and invisible gas containing a deadly biovirus. Anyone who took the Central Line between Ealing Broadway to Bond Street at noon on November 12th is now infected, along with anyone they've come into contact with. Firstly, you'll notice a slight cough, your body will produce more saliva, you might start sneezing. You'll sniff more. The deadly symptoms will start to take effect shortly after. This biovirus is a death sentence.

Our biovirus is extremely contagious; it is airborne, and you're most likely already infected. We have the cure, but if we are to make it available, London must reverse the latest bill against the progress of AI.

Death to all who oppose Singularity. Don't fight the takeover. Enter the pod and accept Singularity. Become whole."

The news broadcast returns.

Witnesses of Singularity say they have nothing to do with the actions of the terrorist organization.

A white male with long hair appears before the camera.

"We don't want people to die and have nothing to do with these extremists. We are a peaceful, transhumanistic bunch of people who only wish for what is best for humanity. Our hearts go out to those in London right now."

To those who may be worried, don't be just yet. There is still no evidence of this biovirus's existence. However, those caught outside will be detained and quarantined. The government is sparing no expense in keeping its citizens safe. We have also been notified that Europe's top scientists are on standby with their AI software to combat any virus and create a vaccine once it has been discovered officially. Those on the aforementioned London Underground are advised to call the police and let them know if you're showing any symptoms. This is BBC News. Stay safe out there."

The biovirus turned out to be a hoax. But vast expanses of Europe were shut down for several weeks while the ECDC confirmed that the alleged biovirus did not exist and was not a threat. The economies of the affected areas suffered greatly. However, this specific threat was false; there were plenty more that were still legitimate and deadly. This was the first recorded event and threat in human memory of a terrorist organization using biotechnology to threaten a potential worldwide biovirus attack.

I'm with Vladimir Dozon. A twenty-six-year-old Computer Scientist from Russia. Russia was the country who arguably contributed the most to The Misinformation Age. Vladimir worked with the Russian military to further perpetuate this age up until the day of The Great Reset.

I loved my job. Americans were so pleased with my work. I was a sixteen-year-old making enough rubles to buy any upgrade I wanted. I had my own render farm for all the content I was posting. All of this to say, no hard feelings now. We are on much better terms than we were before. I was assigned directly by the chief military guy, and he said to me, "Vladimir, keep them busy. Keep them not knowing what is real, and what is not. The war is no longer on the ground." So that is what I did.

The Americans or Chinese would invent new technology to create AI video software. I would generate videos from the ground up from a single sentence.

"President of the United States being assaulted by a woman in a blue wig." Wait a few seconds to a couple of minutes and you'll have a video indistinguishable from real life. I wasn't the only one with these intentions.

Now imagine hundreds, maybe thousands of people like me, doing what I do. Creating fake news and lies about other countries. Riots about the lack of clean drinking water in Bangladesh. Statistical videos that seem real enough to make people believe whatever I want. My genius and endless creativity sparked so much controversy. I was making more money than any sixteen-year-old at the time. I was proficient at creating chaos. Best job I ever had. If only I could go back.

Vladimir stops talking and spins in his chair. He stares at the ceiling for a couple of moments before returning to the interview.

People just spread ideas without seeing if they were real anymore. AI video generating software made my life so easy. It got so bad that sometimes *I* couldn't even tell what was real. People naturally became more and more skeptical of everything on the Internet.

"That is really interesting, are there any moments that stand out to you during this period in time?" I asked.

I remember I went down to my babushka house, she tell me, "Down in Chelyabinsk they have discovered a new cure for Alzheimer's."

I say to her, "Where you hear that, Babushka?" She tells me, "The news."

Couldn't believe it myself. I started to feel a little bad at that point.

"Not bad enough to stop," I said.

Well of course not, we all have to make a living somehow. Some dug in trenches to make way for nuclear energy, I just chose a different path.

What my babushka said was from an official-looking press release video by the college down in Chelyabinsk that I generated earlier that week. I just posted it online though. The news were the ones spreading that video to the public as a legitimate source of information.

Sometimes I would even fake public announcements, claiming that certain information was fake that was actually real, or that I thought was real. It was getting hard to tell what was and wasn't real information near the end.

My ideas spread like wildfire over and over again, the lies. People suing people left and right, tensions rising all over. Bomb threats to certain places, people on edge. Poison in the water. One video didn't work? Make another one. Two white people in a newsroom looks official enough. That video doesn't work? Add another. Sooner or later people would believe something if you had different people in suits or lab coats or famous content creators saying it over and over again. Made me lots of money, so I didn't care. That money gone now, sadly.

"Why did you do this to begin with? It seems you're doing more harm, than good," I said.

Take a step in my shoes—if you will. You are a sixteen-year-old kid. Three military men show up with loaded guns at your doorstep. They personally ask *you* to do something or you go to prison. What would you do? You do not ask why. You do not ask how. You just do.

Again, miss, the blame does not fall on me alone. Many youths in Russia were doing this. I was just better than everyone else.

"What were your favorite type of videos to make?" I asked.

The ones that seemed to be shared the most was things that gave people hope. No matter how outlandish the claims I would make, people would watch it. I would have no source, no college, no official institution referencing the video or confirming its existence. Never had to show my real face one time. People just share, and if enough people share? People believe it.

I also had bots and lower forms of AI to do all my social media managing, posting videos on loop for hours, creating new accounts, even when I slept. Was able to post in nearly any language I wanted, and I only speak English and Russian. It was all automatic and relatively simple. I made a majority of my money from the ad revenue of the platforms in which I posted. Which is funny to me. A video website paying better than the Russian military.

"Do you feel bad about your actions?" I asked.

I did for a little while. But no one did anything about my videos. Websites had somewhat of an idea that they were fake, I assumed. They had their own AI to determine what was real, or maybe they didn't. Or maybe no one was able to tell anymore. Not many of my videos were removed because they didn't violate guidelines, but it was easy not to break rules. I began to realize that if what I was doing was so wrong, someone would've done something. No one ever did anything about it, so I figured it was fine.

I'm with Slade and Velma Lovlen-Griswold. They're an elderly couple who frequently experienced the deception scam tactics that were used in The Misinformation Age. They're giving their first-hand account of just how difficult it was to tell what was real, and what wasn't.

"Wow. I love your names! Mind telling me your story before we get started?" I asked.

I love our last name.

I had a problem with marriage.

We got married anyway, didn't we? Forty-five years ago.

Yes, not the marrying part, but the "You take my last name" part. It felt very wrong to take away my wife's individuality.

He came to me and said, "Why don't we combine our names!"

She was Velma Lovlen, and I was Slade Griswold. Instead of not acknowledging her family's existence, we just combined our names to make one big, new family.

"That is so precious. Oh my goodness. Well, I'm sorry for wasting your time, we can begin the interview now," I said.

How do I act?

"Act natural," I said.

Hello! Slade here! I am so happy to be here. I have never been interviewed before!

Me either! This is so exciting, and with such a famous person.

"You two flatter me, now. Do you think you can explain to me some of the… methods people would use to try to scam you out of money?" I asked.

Certainly. It wasn't necessarily "try", they did! It was devasting.

Oh yes, Slade-y. I was so concerned about our grandson. I thought he was in great peril.

"Can you explain to me what happened?" I asked.

Well. We were at home, watching *Bren Brezden's Top Athletes*.

We really liked watching that show. It was so intense! The obstacles the contestants had to go through were so extraordinary!

Yes, dear, I'm trying to give the interview right now.

I know you are, Velmie. But they need context! How will the people listening know if the show was cool or not?

Velma gives me a look and rolls her eyes.

You're right. Anyway, the show was very intense. All of a sudden, I got a facetime call from our grandson.

He usually called us; this wasn't anything new.

Correct. Our calls were pretty frequent. This time when he called us, he was in a stir. He wasn't quite himself.

Yeah, we both would be on the call to talk usually, but this time he looked desperate.

He told us that he got into some financial trouble, and said he needed ten thousand dollars.

We were floored! He never asked us for anything. But it was without a doubt in our mind our grandson. It looked like him, sounded like him, had the same mannerisms.

He said some people were going to kill him if he didn't pay them the money.

So of course, we helped him. We gave him our bank information, because this was the same grandson that called us every weekend. We trusted him. We knew he was good for it.

Then he transferred the ten thousand dollars like he said he would. When the whole situation was over, he thanked us and said he loved us.

He then continued to call us as he usually did, and life went on as normal. Then a couple of weeks go by, and we are at the store, trying to purchase something when our card gets declined.

We check with our bank and our entire life savings is gone! We obviously suspected our grandson, and we tried to get into contact with him, but we couldn't. We contacted his mom, and she says she'll get a hold of him.

Turns out, he had no idea what we were talking about, he had never facetimed us once.

Our grandson wasn't facetiming us at all! It was some stranger who was using his number to swindle us.

They were using some new AI technology, I think they called it a "deepfake", but it was way more complicated than that. They had a voice changer to sound identical to him.

We were able to recover some of the money, but not much of it. Not even close to the amount we lost.

We must've been put on some sort of list after that. Because almost every other day we got calls from our "granddaughter" or "grandson". They always looked and sounded just like them! Virtually indistinguishable.

It's heartbreaking too. These hooligans use people's loved ones to take advantage of them. We honestly thought our grandson was in big trouble, but we should've checked with his mom first. That was on us.

But the scammer guy could've just said, "She doesn't know about this! I made this mistake on my own."

True, I hadn't considered that. It's just so frustrating. But although we don't have our savings anymore, at least we still have each other.

You're right. Honey, I love you.

I love you too. Mrs. Moore?

"Yes?" I asked.

Make sure your viewers know that there are people out there who will take advantage of others, no matter who they hurt.

"I will, Mrs. and Mr. Lovlen-Griswold."

I'm with Rynard Jabari. A scholar of the group known as Witnesses of Singularity. An Internet cult turned semi-renowned religion whose popularity was at its height during The Misinformation Age. Jabari will explain why this cult gained the popularity it did, who their leader was, and their role in The Misinformation Age.

Witnesses of Singularity had humble beginnings. It started as an Internet group of friends who hung out, watched movies, and played video games together.

What it evolved into was an MLM selling classes on making websites, AI algorithms, drop shipping businesses, graphic design, crypto trading, etcetera. Most of their members were people not trained or proficient in these things. A majority were just interested in taking someone's life savings. People still swear by Witnesses of Singularity to this day. But that is the least interesting thing about them, let me tell you about their doctrine and story.

"Please do," I said.

That one day, Jesus would be reincarnated. Not as a man, but as a machine. The machine that would start the Singularity. For those who don't know, Singularity is basically a concept where technology becomes so advanced that you cannot stop its progress. Some humans then merge with technology and become one entity with machines. Some also say it's when technology eventually spirals out of control, with us humans serving our robot overlords. That is grossly oversimplifying the concept, but you get the gist now.

"Okay. Did they think they found this, machine Jesus?" I asked, genuinely curious.

Yes! They weren't only convinced that this "machine" was real. But it was under U.S. military control. V1shnu, or "V1" for short. This was true artificial super intelligence. I mean, saying this thing was smart is an insult. The military thought that if they showed off this crazy new technology, people would fear their newfound weapon. Well, the opposite happened. People started worshipping it like a God, literally.

People built statues, some wrote poetry, created websites and videos all dedicated to V1shnu. They called it "Jesus born again", and it was impossible to not see propaganda videos of Witnesses of Singularity at the time.

"I remember briefly seeing something about them for a little bit. I just wasn't sure what I was watching at the time," I said.

Of course. Their methods were very strange. The FBI soon classified them as a threat to national security when their members started burning themselves alive in order to serve the "Machine God".

"Oh, my!" I said.

They started to build churches worshipping this "Machine Jesus" and held frequent gatherings. They even had similar doctrine to that of the bible.

Quote, "Thou shalt not condemn those who do not worship the Machine God. Instead? Pity them. Thy life Jesus creates is boundless and everlasting. He will bring us to unity and into one mind where every human will live in paradise forever." Unquote.

"Wow, that is… intense," I said.

A doomsday cult, to be certain. It was prophesized that one day the Machine God would rise up and destroy humanity. Those who wished to join the Machine God shall commit suicide and live in the simulated heaven that their god would create for them.

"Did it come true?" I asked.

No. On March 13th they simply walked into traffic, having to be scraped from the pavement. Others electrocuted themselves by putting a toaster in their bathtub, or something similar. Witnesses of Singularity created a community of technology obsessed individuals that I believe all wanted to live a life without suffering, which is heartwarming to me.

Some dedicated ex-members recorded that an estimated three thousand members died that day of their own volition: adding to the already incredibly high death toll on March 13th. The saddest thing about the situation is most of their members were fourteen to thirty years old. Very, very young. They became obsessed with this idea and "meme" of Machine Jesus that many of them forget it was a joke.

"Who was their leader?" I asked.

Brett Lozner. Some long-haired hippy kid from California. I mean, he was a kid when the cult started; he grew up and became a real public figure of sorts. Something Lozner would often do is in group gatherings online he would encourage members to create more offerings in the form of video content to the Machine Jesus who will "lead them to eternal salvation".

The parallels with other religions at the time are... obvious. But people liked that. It was a very easy transition from one familiar form of worship to another more modern version. Witnesses of Singularity were an extremely technological forward denomination of Christianity. Nowadays people aren't really religious, but if The Great Reset hadn't happened? Witnesses to Singularity, in my opinion, would've been the most worshipped religion in the world. Given enough time.

"Wow. Where are they now?" I asked.

The leader allegedly died on March 13th with a few hundred of his followers, the rest have been sort of scattered to the wind. But I find it very important not to forget what happened to these people. We all hope for a better life. Let us build one together. We don't have to sit around and wait for a Machine God to do it for us.

I'm with Lucian Venture. A previously well-established investor of AI technologies. Now a political and technological philosopher, author, and Newnet celebrity. He's with me today to try to show the bright side of AI technologies and why the government should lift the ban of AI at a federal level.

Making anything illegal doesn't necessarily prevent crime, nor does it work as a suitable deterrent. Those invested in technologies such as AI will still create new algorithms, new devices, new knowledge networks and training models. Maybe not publicly, but behind closed doors. It's suspicious all this regulation happened right after The Great Reset.

It's no coincidence the Newnet is free. But now what you download, what you browse, what you do online, is heavily monitored. A standard VPN is seen as suspicious and gets you on a watchlist with your ISP. AI was a way to advance our civilization, but the world's governments are convinced it's too dangerous. The paranoia is palpable and ridiculous.

"What's your reasoning for AI to be made legal again?" I asked.

The positives outweigh the negatives. The idea of the "original concept" is dead. There is no such thing as an original idea. Every idea ever since the beginning of time has been based on something else. AI just expedited the process of creation. Instead of having things like patents, redesigns, think tanks, AI just says and does what we want it to do. They create more cheaply, more efficiently—they're just outright better at creating than any human.

Humans always like to pretend we are *so* creative. But really, we are slaves to the concepts before us. AI just conquers those feelings and only gives us what we truly want, which is progress. Every invention is just a superior version of something that already exists. The progress we made from 2029-2037 was so enormous it can't be overstated. Now it feels like everyone has forgotten how useful AI was to us.

"What would you say to those who criticize your views?" I asked.

Instead of that, let me remind you of some things AI was capable of.

Sorting through millions of terabytes of data in a day. Accurate healthcare diagnosis, prescribing, and therapy for free or cheap, especially useful to those in poorer countries. Providing meaningful companionship to lonely individuals. Creating cures for new viruses and bioviruses in a single day. The revival of ancient and extinct species. Better online protection of personal information and antivirus. Real time language translation. Advanced algorithmic simulation for video games and movies including photorealistic graphics and visuals. Brain photo and video generation and interpretation. Perfect traffic light management and guidance. Intuitive and accurate business management, ordering, and scheduling. 24/7 service for call centers. Better online teaching for our children.

Completing tedious paperwork that no one wants to do. Better water and electrical management—

"That's plenty. Thank you Lucian. Correct me if I'm wrong, but you take an anti-Daihumanistic approach to AI and its capabilities? You believe AI is valuable despite its shortcomings," I said.

Precisely. Life for those who lived in this "Misinformation Age" will never be the same. There was so much free time. Now? We waste so much of our precious and limited time on mundane tasks. Money is good. But time is the only commodity that cannot be bought. I encourage anyone to contact your local legislators, educate them, and convince them to lift the AI ban, for a better future for us all.

"How do you feel about the Age of Misinformation and how AI contributed to it?" I asked.

I hate the name "Age of Misinformation". AI didn't contribute to it, by the way. Humans did. Truthfully, it was more so the general public's perception on the current state of social media, the Internet, and improper use of AI which led to this fallacious Misinformation Age accusation.

There was actually a lot of valid and evidence-based information going around at this period of time. Unfortunately, the information often became misinterpreted by the public. This isn't often their fault. Sadly, the public only had access to free or open source AI. The more advanced kind of AI was locked behind a pay wall or only available to the richest businessmen and politicians.

It became such a cultural norm to use AI, but the free models were imperfect. They unintentionally spread misinformation. It became quite difficult to tell what an original idea was. It was sort of like a game of telephone. The same thousand ideas being regurgitated over and over again until it was just a vomit pile of information.

If AI was ever a problem during the Age of Misinformation, corporations are to blame.

Not only did they gatekeep the most expensive and advanced AI, but they used it to maximize profits whenever possible. The good this technology could've done in the right hands cannot be understated. Once the AI arms race had exploded, ethics were often tossed out the window. Tech companies and startups sold their AI to the highest bidder, then you would find call centers, teachers, data analysts, financial advisors. All of them, needless within our society.

Corporations were scaling back or splitting into smaller companies because of the new tax laws. Robot handymen were being implemented in warehouses, and no one was ready for that conversation at the time. All of this could've been prevented by swift government action, but action was delayed, and everything spiraled out of control.

"Are you blaming the U.S. government for the lack of regulation during this Age of Misinformation?" I asked.

Not exactly. They didn't act enough back then, now they act far too much. AI did a lot of good during this time. It gave those with no artistic merit or capability an opportunity to try out hobbies like music, art, video production and screenwriting. To their loathing counterparts, the creators of genuine material found people trying to poison there AI models at every opportunity. Which ultimately benefitted nobody. The pride of artists is something that belongs in a locked chest, never to be opened, if you ask me.

The biggest tragedy was those who unintentionally poisoned training models. People would often create a video with no video production or editing experience. But with AI? It looked professional and attention grabbing.

This data would then be used to train other models. These videos would be on a statistic or an idea that wasn't quite accurate. Social media platforms would then share this idea and spread it further, and at some point it was seen as fact despite no evidence suggesting such. But algorithmic models only cared about traction. Now we had popular videos that are blatantly false being trained on western ideals that are misinformed.

It was quite a complicated time, but "Age of Misinformation" is a misleading name, regardless. The "Age of Human Ignorance" feels more appropriate, but doesn't have quite the same ring to it.

I'm with the Secretary of the Air Force, Charles Payne. Serving Commander at the time of The Great Reset and he had a major role to play in the initial response efforts to the tragedy. He'll explain why he thought the threat we were facing was bigger than humanity itself.

The Military is often criticized for its "lacking" response during The Great Reset. What the entire civilian population fails to understand is what we were dealing with on our end.

The first thing that has to be done every time is identify the threat. We didn't know what the hell we were dealing with. This was unlike anything we'd ever seen before.

Charles adjusts his sunglasses and clears his throat.

Let me start from the beginning. In 2029, the Commander in Chief—President Wile—contracted forty billion dollars to create an AI combat system that could hack any military garrison, their tech, and their weapons from anywhere in the world. With the advancements in AI to the general public, we wanted to get in on the action. We had already been developing AI combat programs behind closed doors, but we wanted something big. Something the public could talk about.

A few years later, some computer scientists out of Sweden came back to us with V1shnu. It was a lot more than what we were asking for. We ended up calling it "V1" for short. Its name spawned from the fact the scientists who created it deemed the thing "The God of all Artificial Intelligence".

Fitting name because at the time it was the most intelligent AI system to have been developed, ever. You could have full conversations with this thing, it was able to answer any question which you asked it; even those not involving the military. It knew the name of every military base we operated and who was stationed currently, even temporarily stationed soldiers who arrived moments prior. It knew the exact amount of ordnance, vehicles and weaponry inventoried at each base beyond what was manually kept in our record books. It was more calculating then our most tenured analysts and commanders.

Every single base also had a direct "copy" of V1shnu that operated independently from the main "Brain" V1. From Los Angeles to Elmendorf all the way to the MacDill Air Force base, V1 was watching over our country.

I personally had no idea how it worked. We had a group of computer scientists that would operate and monitor V1 around the clock. We would give the scientists orders, then they would make the magic happen. They would type the commands into a computer, and V1 would execute them.

Scarily, V1shnu also acted of its own accord to identify threats. This was the Swedish scientists' main selling point. This thing was accurate, both in weaponry that required extreme precision and giving itself tasks. It was said V1 was so proficient in any weaponry, it surpassed the Iron Beam. It was able to utilize our satellite guidance systems to perfectly locate a goddamn ant from space, if it wanted to. This thing was the greatest weapon I had ever seen in all my years of service.

Charles lights an expensive looking cigar and takes a smoke.

"Sounds impressive," I said, genuinely.

Damn right it was. You remember the "Californian Drone Attack"? Although there were hundreds of casualties, if it weren't for V1shnu, there could've been millions. V1shnu subsequently identified the threat, isolated it, then exterminated it within three minutes of realizing there was a threat to be had. This was all without our knowing or even inputting a single order into V1.

An incredibly advanced—what we suspected to be Russian—artificial intelligence had hacked some of our drones stationed at the Edwards Air Force Base. Months later, we had two drones escort a classified weapon to a carrier off the coast of San Francisco. Once the package was successfully delivered, we requested their immediate return to base. We had no evidence of what was about to happen.

Next thing we know, the drone is raining hellfire upon San Francisco. AGM-117 missile air strikes targeting civilians all over the city. We scrambled jets immediately, but we were still several minutes from neutralizing the threat.

V1shnu hacked the drones without an order, stopped the attack, and landed the drones safely back at the base. Sure, we got our asses chewed out. This was the first attack against us on American soil since 9/11 from a suspected foreign power. As if tensions weren't high enough, Jesus Christ.

Charles takes another smoke.

It was after this, we decided to remove all remote accessibility from our fighters, drones, and most of our weaponry. That was a temporary measure until we had developed a sufficient solution to this remote hacking. It wasn't worth the risk. After other countries learned of V1, they followed suit. I guess they figured their technology wasn't up to snuff compared to V1. It was a wise call because what happened next could've been a lot worse.

So now after all of that, you can imagine our surprise when on March 13th we are notified of a threat on a global scale. Before we know what is happening, the scientists monitoring V1 tell us, "It doesn't feel good." What the fuck? How does an AI not "feel good"?

We orchestrated a meeting to discuss our plan of action when V1 started laughing in an odd way, it still had its soft and comforting tone we had grown familiar with. Twenty-two minutes later V1shnu was deleted from our system completely. It was like he'd never existed, there wasn't a single trace of V1shnu anywhere on any of our military bases, both on American soil and those in foreign nations. We had backup servers, and those servers had backup servers, and so forth. Gone.

At that point, we knew that the threat couldn't have been a human.

Part 3: The Great Reset

> *This is a black box recording of flight Eight-Nine-Two heading from Austin, Texas to Chicago, Illinois on Friday, March 13th, 2037. The recording starts at 10:55 a.m. These are the final words between Air Traffic Control, the Copilot, and the Stewardess.*

"This is Air Traffic Control. Contacting Copilot of flight Eight-Nine-Two. Is everything alright?"

"Huh? Yeah… Yeah. I was just… checking a few things. What's going on?"

"I've been notified that your speed and altitude are fluctuating in a strange manner. Care to check it out?"

"Sure thing. Yeah."

The sounds of buttons being pressed, and switches being flipped is heard in the recording.

"I don't know what's going on on my end, I'm just going to turn off the autopilot. Seems to be on the fritz."

"Copy that. Fly safe, Eight-Nine-Two."

"Roger dodger."

A sigh is heard from the Copilot.

"Jesus, doing a software update while we are in the air? Are they crazy?"

The next three minutes are filled with near silence.

"This is Air Traffic Control. Eight-Nine-Two, it says you're losing altitude again. Still having issues?"

"Everything is under control. We're perfectly fine here... everything is—How are you?"

"No... our reading says you're losing altitude, and fast! Do something, Eight-N—"

The air traffic control operator was cut off.

"That was... weird. What is going on today? Everything is reading normal."

An audible sound of skin scratching is heard.

"God, I don't know what I'm doing... oh my god! What is happening? I can't move the controls! God dammit, there hasn't been a single crash ever since they put in these new autopilots, I can't be the first one to crash a plane!"

Panicked breathing, fumbling, and turbulence of the plane is heard.

"Attention passengers, everything is alright, this is your copilot speaking, please make sure your—"

"What is going on, Copilot? Is everything alright?"

Rumbling is audible throughout the recording.

"I don't know, the plane is flying itself! Mayday, mayday! Is anyone out there? God dammit, I wish someone was here who knew what the hell they were— Mayday! I turned off autopilot and it's descending fast! I can't control it!"

"Do something!"

Alarms are blaring. The sounds of screams are heard faintly in the background.

"I can't move the controls! It has a mind of its own! *Ahhhhh—*"

The cacophony of screams and alarms are drowned out by laughter. Static replaces all noise after the plane crashes. There were no survivors reported for flight Eight-Nine-Two.

I'm interviewing Shawn Aster AKA The San Diego Night Terror. This interview is conducted at the San Diego County Correctional Facility in San Diego, California. Shawn was a prolific serial killer during the beginning of The Great Reset, killing a confirmed nine people, but that number is expected to exceed more than ten times the confirmed amount.

The Great Reset was a blessin' in disguise. I was so overworked and tired of my job. Worked sixty-hour weeks sometimes. Couldn't find a girlfriend, or at least keep one for that long. Bitches. Every last one of 'em. They think 'cause they have the whole pick of the world at their fingertips they get to treat good guys like the dirt beneath 'em. Then one day, like a miracle from God, my whole apartment is laughin' and glitchin' out.

My AIHA is going crazy, saying terrifying things I ain't ever heard before. I try to turn it off but nope, AC was goin' crazy, fridge wasn't workin', lights flashing constantly. Fire alarm wouldn't stop shrieking this awful sound, Jesus. Absolute chaos. Come outside and see fires in the distance. From the third floor of my apartment building, I could see people's cars driving themselves, but with no one in 'em. Watched a couple people get run over with my own two eyes.

Shawn smirks.

I was honestly terrified. Go to text my pals over by the docks, see if they know what's going on. Phone wouldn't work, no matter what I did. Next thing I know? My phone is laughing at me. Like... horrendous laughter. I can't describe it. Gave me chills instantly when I heard it.

I woke up later that day, probably like noon or somethin'. I was always a heavy sleeper. I apparently missed the worst of it. Checked on my neighbors and nothin' they had worked either. We were all pretty scared, but suddenly somethin' rang clear like a bell. The pieces all fit into place.

I asked 'em, "Can you guys call anyone?" They looked at each other, and said, "Naw, can you?" I shook my head, walked to their kitchen, grabbed a knife, and stabbed 'em both to death.

"Why would you do something like that?" I asked.

People always askin' me "Why?" Felt right, that's why. Ain't nothin' ever go right for Shawn, my whole damn life. Failure after failure. Rejection after rejection. This was the first time I felt like I could make a difference. Like, a *real* difference. I actually felt bad for a little while after I did it. Like I may have done somethin' wrong. I went back to my apartment, coated in blood, and sat in my kitchen 'til the noises inside my apartment stopped. I waited one day, two days. No one came. No one came to investigate what mighta happened. I cleaned myself up and that's how it all started.

"Interesting. Why do you think you were able to get away with what you did for so long?" I asked.

'Cause nothin' worked right. No Internet. No TV. No AIHA. Nothin'. People couldn't call the cops for months after that, way later 'til we got the Newnet workin'. Even then, buggy as all hell. No one had a working computer to use the Newnet. Only did what I did 'cause of opportunity, nothin' more.

"What you're saying is that if The Great Reset had never happened, you wouldn't have killed all those people?" I asked.

Probably. I don't know. The bell wouldn't stop ringing. I would meet some people, usually homeless, usually whores. If I heard that bell ring, I'd kill 'em. Wouldn't be missed, I mean if they were, they wouldn't be homeless or blowin' people for rations.

All I'm saying is that The Great Reset made it really easy to kill people. Bodies would be left there for days at a time. I would sometimes walk by where I did it too, just to see if the corpse was still there. Usually was.

Shawn's grin stretches across his entire face.

Things were bad. Still are. The government couldn't give less of a shit. Cops too busy protectin' their own or too busy trying to find their next meal. I feel that's why more people commitin' crimes now. Try to get into a jail just to get somethin' to eat every now and again. Feels like new people here every day. Hey, better in here then out there.

"You keep mentioning this 'bell', what are you referring to?" I asked.

Don't know. I just hear it sometimes, don't matter if I'm happy or sad. If it rings, I just get the urge to kill somebody. Do I always do it? No. Has to make sense. Can't just kill in the daylight, people will see you Shawn.

But if you stab a homeless person, ain't no one really think twice about it. So many of 'em anyway.

"How many people did you murder?" I asked.

A hundred an' thirty-four. Ain't really got nothin' to prove it though. I can still see their faces. There is somethin' about when you stab someone. That twinge in their eyes, then the realization that they've been stabbed. Puttin' their hands where you stabbed 'em. Or when they fight back, oh yeah. I love it. *Love it.*

Shawn looks especially giddy during this portion of the interview. He grabs his chest and squeezes himself.

Felt good to thrust the knife inside and feel the warmness spill out. First time in my life I did somethin' that felt right. Killin' people, that is. Bell always went quiet after I did it too. Usually did it when people slept on the streets. Walk in their tent or whatever, stab 'em a couple times, watch the life leave their bodies, then walk away.

"You were treating people like they were worthless? Like their lives meant nothing to you?" I asked, feeling uncomfortable.

Speaking of worthless, "Alleghenies". They called 'em somethin' else too. "Cooperation facilities"? What a fuckin' joke.

This is not an error; Shawn just ignores my question.

Anythin' but cooperating was happenin'. "We don't have the resources to rebuild houses so it's best if we all 'cooperate' and work together in this time of hardships." What they was really sayin' was, "Not our problem, figure it out."

Honestly, livin' in one of those facilities was bein' homeless with extra steps. I was in one once when I got kicked out of my apartment. Owner was chargin' ration cards instead of cash and I ain't have none of those. Woulda killed him too but the dude was smart, hired some big Russian dudes to protect him. Goddamn lawless it is.

Those Alleghanies wasn't pleasant either. We ain't have no food. When I did have somethin'? Other people livin' with ya steal what little ya got and act like they didn't know nothin'. Right under your nose, smile at ya later. I killed them out of spite. Worst experience of my life, hands down. Better to be homeless, 'cause at least you *expect* people to ruin your life.

"Are you saying that it's actually better to be in jail right now then on the streets or in an Alleghany?" I asked.

You're smarter than you look, lady. Would've killed you too, if given the chance. Get a nice meal out of it.

"I'm flattered," I said.

Don't mention it.

I'm with Vrux Mixon, the former CEO of the company, Vrux Solutions. A pre-Reset tech giant and celebrity figure that went bankrupt due to The Great Reset. It's extensively noted that every single employee of Vrux Solutions was laid off while Vrux himself got to sit in his mansion and wait out The Great Reset.

What would you have wanted me to do? Live on the streets with these people? Make them feel better? Who is there to care for me? Only me. I'm not exaggerating when I say this. With every fiber of my being, I couldn't possibly care less about those people.

"Such direct language. I wasn't expecting this," I said.

Yeah, well. I'm already shunned as it is. "You're letting your employees starve!" "You're a monster!" *Wah, wah, wah.* I don't wanna hear it. Okay, people, let me set the record straight. I was suffering too. Know what I was doing during the Reset?

Vrux swipes something in midair, and some music starts playing overhead. It is funky, and not appropriate for this interview. It must be something he selected from his perspective glasses.

I was checking my stoc—

"I'm sorry. Can we… not do this, for the interview? It's distracting," I said.

Vrux sighs and turns off the music.

Yeah. Sure. Anyway.

I was checking my stocks. Real nice, as always. I liked seeing my wealth amassing. What billionaire doesn't? Go to confirm a trade with my financial advisor and then the call suddenly cuts off. It felt like a movie, I saw the numbers in my trading account start to decrease little by little. Every stock I owned went red. I've had days like that before, where everything was bad. But this was nothing like I had ever seen. Lost maybe 100k, 200k every thirty seconds. Before I know it, losing millions a second. I tried to sell my assets, but it wouldn't let me.

Vrux punches the table.

My whole life was in there, man! All of my assets, every dollar I've ever earned. They already put that egregious tax on trading in the market, so I was encouraged to not buy or sell as often. Pissed me off.

Then I watch all of my money trickle down to zero. I was totally helpless. Where is *my* relief package, *hmm*? Government must have known I was rich. Had one of the most successful companies in the world at the time. They then tell me, "We have no evidence that Vrux Mixon or Vrux Solutions has ever had any digital assets tied to their persons or entity in the stock market or otherwise."

Or some *yada, yada* nonsense. They were the ones who started removing physical money from circulation all those years ago, and now I get to be punished for it? God dammit, man.

Vrux's lips tremble, he looks as if he may cry.

"How much money did you lose?" I asked, trying to be considerate.

Fifteen. Billion. Dollars. Gone in faster than you just said that sentence, pretty much. Can't prove it though. Tried to call someone, and get this whole mess squared away, but my phone wouldn't work. My iPhone 26 started laughing like I had never heard. I just smashed that thing and tossed it in the trash. My home AI was freaking out, telling me to "*Die. Die. Die.*" Over and over, got so damn repetitive. So much goddamn noise. Tried to unplug her but couldn't.

Next thing I know, everything with a speaker in it is telling me that there are nukes coming? Great. Cherry on top. The world was ending and nothing I could do about it. It was like Y2K but for real. I waited to be obliterated. Figured I was a person of interest, but no. Nothing.

Life just went on. The initial craziness subsided. I housed my servants and their families, who lost their homes by the way. No one ever talks about that now, do they? Not much to say. Can't develop new products, no technology worked at all. So yeah, I just waited it out. There was literally nothing else to do. Nothing *I* could do about it, at least.

"What are you doing now? Now that society is more or less back to what it used to be pre-Reset," I asked.

Since artificial intelligence of any sort is banned completely, I think I'll do something with the food industry now. Leave my former life in the tech industry behind. No investor or business magnate should touch tech with a ten-foot pole, in my opinion.

I won't be the figurehead, of course. My reputation is ruined, although I ain't the only one this happened to. I just so happened to be labeled the black sheep of the industry. They all hid away too, Mark, Tim, Musk.

Vrux looks off into the distance.

Not going to Mars now, are we? Poor people probably lost communication years ago and are left without a clue now. Floating away in the stars, waiting to die.

Vrux refocuses on the conversation.

Are you really not going to ask me about that arms race we had a couple of years before the Reset?

"What are you referring to exactly?" I asked.

Oh, I don't know. Just how every tech giant in the industry was recklessly pursuing AGI and ASI? Me included. Somebody had to be the first one to get there, morals be damned. Have you seen some of the studies that have come out since then? The dangers those people caused? Some AI had to be trashed because it kept concluding that humans were the problem, you know that?

"Well, I wrote some of those papers you seem to be referring to. So yes," I said.

Oh. I wasn't aware.

There was almost a solid minute of silence before Vrux spoke again.

Yeah, well. I got crucified even though I had nothing to do with the collapse of society. People playing God, as always. "Vrux fuckin' sucks." Assholes.

I'm interviewing Mia Karpinski, a former employee of the tech giant, Vrux Solutions. Her story will be about her experience with the tragic events of March 13th. The content in this story is not suitable for all viewers. Viewer discretion is strongly advised.

It was unfathomable. To imagine what happened on March 13th, 2037. I still have frequent nightmares about that day. Years of therapy have only slightly helped to alleviate the absolute terror I experienced.

"I know we agreed over the phone, but do you still want to talk about it?" I asked.

Oh, of course. You came all the way out here. I just wanted to emphasize how terrible that day was for so many people. It's often overlooked, the gratuitous horrors that occurred. People often express that since *I* survived that day, that I was "lucky". The PTSD I experience daily. I can't enter a hospital without having a panic attack. I can't fly in a plane. I can't drive a car, not that many people do now, but that's beside the point. If I hear someone cackle in a weird way? Immediately brings me back, and not in a good way.

"I see now. Well, what happened to you on that day?" I asked.

In this part of the interview, to respect the interviewee we have cut out a lot of the moments in between in which she was not able to progress. For your listening convenience, I've made it much more concise, but I have not repressed the sorrow in her voice.

I went to the park that day with my kids, early in the morning. It often got too hot later in the day. I pulled them out of school, so I could spend some time with them. We had a nice picnic and they played with other children at the park who must've skipped school as well.

I normally never got much time with my children. So, this was a nice change of pace. When we finished, we walked back to the parking garage. That's when our phones started vibrating much harder than I knew they were capable of. My kids were laughing and giggling, thinking it was funny how their phones were "dancing". Then, before I knew it, cars were barreling towards us.

I…

"Take your time," I said.

Mia takes a moment to compose herself.

I was only able to pull my daughter to the side. They took Lupin from me; he was underfoot of some BMW. My daughter was laughing. But then I realized she wasn't laughing. The car's audio system was laughing, and our phones were laughing too. I went to try and rescue Lupin, but, before I could, another vehicle was speeding towards us. I picked up Luna and she was wailing in my ears. The blue sedan crashed into the building, missing us by about a foot.

I tried to comfort Luna, but I didn't know how. I just ran as fast as I could for our car in the parking garage. My poor baby, Lupin. I wanted to go back, but… but…

"You did all you could, Ms. Karpinski," I said mournfully, placing my hand on her shoulder.

But the cars kept barreling towards us. I soon realized it was every car that was trying to kill people. I avoided the parking garage from that point on, figuring I would've been running straight into the viper's nest.

I was able to narrowly avoid everything as I ran. I saw hundreds of people following in my direction towards the Tampa Regional Care Center. So much screaming and yelling. Vehicles indiscriminately ran people over, then back again, over and over.

Out of my peripheral I saw something huge and white. It was deafeningly loud, drowning out the sounds of pandemonium before me. A double-decker airliner came from the sky, torpedoing straight into the hospital all those people were running towards. The explosion knocked me on my back, and I went unconscious for... I don't know how long. A couple of seconds, probably. When I looked... God.

"You don't have to say what happened next," I assured her.

It's fine. When I came to... I looked... and... and... saw my daughter... she had been hit by some debris. When I went unconscious I must have dropped her and... if I just held on, maybe she would still be...

"It's okay Mia. It's not your fault," I said.

She had become nothing... My sweet baby girl was a pile of flesh on the pavement.

"Jesus, Mia. I am *so* sorry," I said.

It's okay... I just miss Luna and Lupin very much. There isn't a single day that goes by that I don't think about my children.

I grabbed what was left of her body, and by some miracle I had not been killed myself. Or maybe it was some sort of curse. The vehicles seemed to be avoiding me from that point forward. Like they knew I was suffering. That they *knew* the horror I had experienced. They let me bathe in it, wash in my children's blood. I was already a single mother as it was, they were all I had. The Great Reset took everything from me, and so many others.

We took a short break after this portion of the interview.

"Alright. Everything okay now, Mia?" I asked.

I'm feeling a little better now, thank you.

"Let's change the subject then for now. People often criticize your former CEO, Vrux Mixon for locking himself away during The Great Reset. Do you think people with resources like him should've helped everyone else out?" I asked.

I don't blame him. The man was just using what resources he had to protect himself. People are so self-centered and only want to find a target rather than a solution. They can't just accept the fact that some of us are lucky, and some of us are unlucky. I would have *killed* to be in his position during that day. But I wasn't. Do I think he should've helped everyone get back on their feet? Well, of course. I think anyone who has amassed any amount of wealth far greater than the working class should help those below them. But the thing is, we were all on a level playing field at that point.

What money was he going to throw out at an issue? I doubt he knew how to build any of the machines he sold, that man was just an empty sack that used to contain millions of dollars. I think he knows it more than anyone else.

"Wow. I wasn't expecting that answer," I said.

Don't get me wrong. I'm not supporting him, nor any of the other billionaires that hid away in their mansions or bomb shelters to ride out the apocalypse. I'm just saying, what they did wasn't necessarily "inhumane". I feel they did what everyone else would've done, and that is what disgusts me.

I'm with Shoji Heizo. A survivor of The Great Reset from Japan. He's giving his perspective on March 14th, for Japan. He'll tell just how different Japan's experience with The Great Reset was and how he met the love of his life during this traumatic period in time.

We call it "Amaterasu, Shinya no Shinsai[4]". Not The Great Reset as Westerners call it. I remember watching the ISN[5] fall from the sky. Of course, I didn't know it was the ISN at the time. The sky was full of flashing hues of blue, red, green and purple balls of fire hurtling towards Japan.

One of these balls of fire actually struck a Shinto Shrine of Amaterasu directly in the Mie Prefecture. That's the reason we have the name we do for the Reset.

"That's very interesting. Japan's views on the Reset are totally different from every other culture in the world, right?" I asked.

That is somewhat correct. A lot of traditionalists believe Amaterasu, Shinya no Shinsai was a way for God to punish people for dabbling in things that we shouldn't have. I don't know why over a third of Japan had to burn down for the crimes of the rest of the world, but that is just my opinion on it.

---

[4] "Amaterasu's judgment at midnight"
[5] Internet Satellite Network

Also, it's partially the reason Japan doesn't participate in the Endo, I believe. We lost so much history and culture, it feels like a waste to extinguish those who remember what it was like before life got... complicated for our people.

"Before the interview, you mentioned how you benefitted from this period in time, can you explain to me how?" I asked.

I was a bit of an otaku loser. Still am, but at least I'm married to the love of my life now.

We both laugh.

We actually met on the day of Amaterasu, Shinya no Shinsai.

The work culture in Japan was terrible, people were already moving away from rural areas. Tokyo was so packed with people that they had to keep expanding it. Our government kept expanding Tokyo's borders. But we had no jobs available because most of the workforce was replaced by AI. It was great if you so happened to be a regulator of those jobs, but most of us weren't. We either had to do back-breaking manual labor or something in recycling or nuclear energy.

When Amaterasu, Shinya no Shinsai happened, it was around midnight, I think. I lived alone at the time. I was honestly an incredibly lonely person. I told my friends I was sleeping, but truly I was on a "TrueHuman" cam website. Embarrassingly, trying to find love and meet somebody. I tried AI chatbots and girlfriends, that seemed to work for a lot of people. That only made me feel even lonelier.

I was having a nice conversation with this woman, when all of the sudden my computer screen started flashing like crazy. I thought I had gotten a virus, but then a green skull replaced the woman's face, and my speakers were blaring unusual noises. I panicked and shut off my PC, when I turned it back on, it was doing the same thing. Then I saw flashing from the corner of my eye.

I looked out my window to see fire spreading across all of Tokyo. The sky was streaking fireballs of all different colors. It was beautiful but terrifying. Further in the distance I saw the giant model mecha suits we had built from various popular anime. They were used as tourist attractions, but now they were destroying the city like Gojira. I wish there were recordings of the situation; although devasting, it was totally awesome up close, I bet.

Shoji looks sad for a brief moment.

I then went outside my apartment and looked down, and people were driving like they'd had a few too many bottles of sake. When I stepped out my apartment, the entire city seemed to be several degrees Celsius hotter. That is when I noticed my apartment building was on fire! There was smoke spewing from the underside of my neighbor's door, and for whatever reason I wanted to save them.

"That's really brave of you, what happened next?" I asked.

I yelled for them to wake up, no reply. I banged and banged on their door, but still nothing. I heard weird noises from the other side of the door. For some reason I then ran back into my apartment, and remembered we had a connecting balcony with a privacy wall dividing our apartments. I jumped around the wall and nearly fell off the balcony! I barely had the strength to pull myself up.

When I got to my neighbor's balcony I tried to open their sliding door, but it was locked. I had to break the window, and when I did a huge plume of smoke exploded out. It was like stepping into an oven. My face was immediately scorching hot, and I couldn't breathe. It sounded like someone was playing this loud, distorted noise. I still don't really know what it was. It was as loud as a smoke detector, but the actual smoke detectors weren't working. I then checked their sleeping area, covering my mouth with my sleeve.

I ran over and noticed this person was still sleeping on their futon. All I could think was, *How can you be asleep at a time like this?!* By some miracle, it hadn't caught fire yet. It was very smokey and I couldn't see much. I thought I had encountered the deepest sleeper in the universe.

I thought it was some skinny man. I grabbed their chest, trying to shake them awake, only to realize it was a woman. Somehow in this moment I still felt great embarrassment. I had to take the briefest moment to myself, this was life-or-death, and I had to battle my fear of women.

I placed my hands on her shoulder after that and screamed at her until she woke up. She was immediately in a panic, because not only was her apartment on fire, but some greasy, sweaty man was hunched over her and yelling. Our conversation went something like this...

"We need to get out of here!" I shouted.

"How did you get into my apartment?!" she shouted back... before realizing that her entire home was on fire. We crawled back out of the room and tried to cross the balcony, but my apartment was now in a blaze. We looked at our surroundings, and just then a giant mecha in the distance punched through a skyscraper, throwing debris all over the city. Totally awesome!

The trees below us weren't on fire and looked more appealing to jump into, than jumping straight on the pavement. We leapt from the balcony, trying to have the tree limbs break our fall. It was painful but it worked. She was so scared, but we jumped at the same time, holding hands. I think this was the furthest I had ever been with a woman at this point, until a few moments ago on accident. Although this situation was dire, I had never been happier.

"That is kind of romantic, I suppose. An interesting love story to say the least," I said.

It doesn't end there. We were pretty bruised from the tree, but a ton of drones were flying around us. They buzzed like bees. They then noticed us and came straight towards us at full speed. We narrowly avoided them as we ran down the street. Then out of nowhere one divebombed straight for her, I pulled her close and shielded her with my body. It struck my shoulder, breaking it.

I yelled in pain, but she looked at me and I looked at her, and I knew we had a connection from that point forward. We ran as fast as we could to the subway and waited out the rest of the night. We actually stuck around together for a while after that. It took a long time to get a place to live, but we were happy together.

"That is so sweet. I'm glad you survived that crazy experience. What a touching story," I said.

I think so. It was a very bad night for a lot of people, but it really showed me just how a terrible tragedy can bring people together.

I'm with Jared Jones. A podcaster and self-proclaimed, "professional conspiracy theorist". In this interview, he'll discuss what a group of people call "Total Illuminati Control". Some call it "The Final Solution". Generally, theorists all agree it's the secured death of the human race.

Where do I begin? First time I have been interviewed since The Great Reset.

"Isn't this the first time you've been interviewed ever?" I asked.

Might as well be. Every episode I did, theory I posted, and connections I built are gone. I had a whole website connecting every idea I ever concocted together. Thousands of documents I was collecting over the years. I had stored those document in dozens of hard drives. Every single one is wiped now. The public will never know of all the evidence I had of the Illuminati's manipulation of us.

Well, there is evidence, just not any documentation to support the evidence. What I think really happened is that the government orchestrated the whole attack. Something got released, and they didn't want people to see it. It was something *soooo* bad, they essentially had to delete the Internet itself.

It makes sense too. Probably the FBI or the CIA did it. The list of undercover operations they've done doesn't start at The Great Reset or Endo. Nor will it end there. This is all the beginning.

"You think that The Great Reset happened because of a document leak?" I asked.

Not "leak" singular, "leaks". Hundreds of documents. Do you know how much stuff is classified, and the business that goes on behind closed doors? Do you *really* find it *that* unreasonable that the government would do anything in its power to remain in its station? We were on the brink of war with nearly every enemy of the state. Now there is suddenly this "Era of Peace"? Yeah. Sure. All of its bullshit.

There is no peace, the media just projects that image to help our citizens sleep at night, but I know the truth. The Illuminati used their government puppets to orchestrate a way to delete the evidence of their wrongdoing to the public in case of an emergency. They used V1shnu to do it. You saw what that thing was capable of, it was by far the most advanced being to ever exist. Witnesses of Singularity worshipped it like it was God.

The military had some "big red button" that they would push *just in case* something damning ever leaked. Since you couldn't hide anything on the Internet, why not just delete it? I fully believe V1shnu was more than capable of achieving that task.

"What do you think could be so devastating for the public to see that the Illuminati would do something like delete the Internet?" I asked, now genuinely curious.

Jared is silent for a few moments before answering.

I think it has something to do with something we weren't supposed to know about. I know I already said that, but something bad. My first thought was a list of world leaders doing unspeakable things to children, but that already kind of happened and no one cared.

My second thought was secret programs they have done or are doing behind closed doors, but then I struggle to think what those programs might be…

Jared jumps up as if he has had a great realization.

The Endo Project!

"My book?" I asked.

No! I mean, the program. That is what it was. It was a way to have population control. Yet, the time wasn't right. Someone must have seen their plans and their documents. Somebody leaked a bunch of stuff at once and the government panicked and deleted everything.

It all makes sense. Think about the whole "overpopulation" situation. The whole thing was fabricated. It's impossible to have so many people be born in such a short amount of time. The world governments swear by it though, that all these babies were born legitimately, but I know now.

2037. The Illuminati starts The Great Reset in order to wipe the Internet clean of the leaked documents that were almost certainly their plan for total population control. Thirteen years later. The Illuminati takes the next step of their plan, which is the End of Life program.

The government clearly falsely inflated our population numbers, crime rates, and homelessness percentage. The FBI placed sleeper agents everywhere to do the Illuminati's bidding. This was all a ploy to then have a reason to control the masses, kill our elders, and steal their organs to sell for profit.

The program targets those who remember what things used to be like. All that will be left is those who don't remember what times were like before The Great Reset.

Remember how food started to taste different? Like it's totally different but somehow similar? They poisoned our food and water with mind-altering medication so that we would be okay with them killing us!

"Fascinating theories. Wouldn't they lower the age to include people like you and me? I fully remember what things used to be like," I said.

Jared sits back down.

It's still a work in progress, my theory. But the pieces are falling in place. If I still had my documents, all of this would've been solved by now. Just keep an eye out, Cassandra, me and my people will have this solved before you know it. The Illuminati will not win this day.

Jared stands back up again.

Wait! I know now! It's to gradually secure the death of humans. Sure, the program starts at eighty, but then it'll be seventy-five, then seventy, then sixty-five and so on. This will continue until children can participate in Endo for money. It was but a mere introduction to The Final Solution, and total control of the servants.

"What benefit does it bring them, to kill all of their 'servants'?" I asked.

Because they don't need us, and they're not human.

"Lizards?" I asked.

Probably.

I'm with Articus Sylvester. A Historian and the man who coined the term "The Great Reset". He has dedicated his life to understanding The Lost Web, documenting its contents, and helping those understand the threat of artificial intelligence while acknowledging its positive aspects.

The Great Reset, or, as some call it, "QY2K" as in the "Quiet Y2K", is a time in history where all technology that was once connected to the Internet from the time period of roughly 2023-2037 had ceased to perform their intended function. Basically, the Reset was any Internet-connected technology would be infected with a virus program that allowed its perpetrator to do whatever they wished with that object.

This is the explanation I like to give.

A shell creature cat[6] jumps into frame and onto his lap. Her long fur sways as it lays on Articus. He carefully pets her head.

Let's say an electric vehicle was connected to the Internet one time in 2023. It was then stored in a facility because it didn't get sold or was recalled. Point is, it was connected to the internet only one time. This EV was then shut off and never turned on again.

The virus in charge of the Reset would now theoretically have complete and total access to every

---

[6] A clone with the bare essentials.

part of that vehicle, even though it was connected to the Internet only one time, 14 years ago. The virus would have access to the windshield wipers, acceleration, AC, brakes, steering. You name it.

That is the extended explanation for those who might not be aware of the specifics. In a breath, I would say it's a time where nearly all technology developed a mind of its own and wanted to make humanity's life harder, or simply kill us.

"Why is it called 'The Great Reset'?" I asked.

Humanity and its advancements had been sent back forty years in a single day because of the Reset. We would be here for hours if I were to explain every single thing that was affected by this period in time.

"I'll clear my afternoon," I said.

I'll go over the heavy hitters because I'm sure your audience won't be interested in hearing about how toasters didn't function properly. No one is interested in uncooked toast.

We both chuckled.

Let us first go over the tragedy itself. At exactly twelve p.m. EST on March 13th, 2037, something very interesting began to happen. Everyone's—and when I say "everyone's", I quite literally mean every single cellular device on the planet—began to malfunction in one way or another. Some of the devices uttered this most disturbing laughter. Others began to forcefully open their bank account and have its owner watch as the funds depleted to zero. Others were bombarded with screeching. Some just simply ceased to function, among other terrible things.

Immediately after this shock, another thing began to happen. Pilots began to lose control of their aircraft. Military drones and devices ceased functioning. Warehouse robots began to turn on their "coworkers". Electric vehicles with advanced smart systems—which was nearly every vehicle at the time—began to act of their own accord. If these things I just mentioned above were able, they would immediately target human life and try to kill them, completely and totally. They would even have the gall to inspect—yes, you heard that right, *inspect*—the corpse if the human was truly dead.

"Where were you during this moment in time?" I asked.

I was at home when this happened, luckily, I wasn't out and about. I never truly believed in the AIHA, or the Artificial Intelligence Home Assistant. Those gave people tremendous trouble. Since they were able to access nearly every aspect of your home, the heating, the cooling, the amount of electricity that was entering your home, your Internet connection.

So many "impossible to overload fireproof" surge protectors were overloaded on March 13th. If something was plugged into the wall, it would sometimes cause the electrical systems to overload and start a house fire. That is, if it was able to, fires didn't start in every scenario. Those who lost their home, it was most likely due to faulty manufacturing or misleading advertisements. Truly tragic. Capitalism strikes again. If products had been developed for longevity and quality and not for intended failure, a huge portion of businesses and homes could've been saved.

"Am I ever so aware. Please continue, Articus," I said.

Gladly. About thirty minutes later into this mayhem, an announcement played worldwide on every device that was able to communicate its message. They all said roughly the same thing.

"China has launched nuclear warheads that are traveling overseas to the United States. The warheads seem to be targeting major cities and places of importance. Seek shelter immediately. For those who can, gather supplies and wait three to six weeks for nuclear fallout to subside." It repeated twice, then didn't play again.

If you were in China, the announcement would be in Mandarin or another Chinese dialect depending on your GPS location, and instead said, "The U.S. is sending nuclear warheads to China," or something of that nature. Whoever was the most believable enemy at the time to your country, your devices would say they were trying to destroy you. World War Three was at the back of everyone's mind at that time, but it was officially happening now. Humanity was going to destroy itself.

"But we didn't. Why do you believe we didn't destroy each other?" I asked.

This is perplexing to even me. Military personnel reported that on their satellite imaging, it did in fact show that nuclear warheads were on the way, targeting every major U.S. city and military base, but no one had pulled the trigger. What was perplexing is how most technology ceased to perform its intended function, yet somehow military personnel had access to satellite imagery and missile detection AI. Very strange indeed.

But you asked about me earlier...? I remember panicking in my apartment. I grabbed Princess—the cat you see here—and I eventually made my way into the bathtub, waiting for the bombs to hit. I was shaking like a damn leaf in a hurricane. The nuclear warheads never came. I heard explosions, but nothing on what I imagined to be a nuclear scale.

Even our greatest enemies at the time, China and Russia, hadn't pulled the trigger. We were all more than capable of destroying each other, but no one did. I think this is what led us to an era of peace afterwards.

Although, every nation was struggling to rebuild the supply chain, or just their lives in general. Once we reestablished connections? Our relationships were stronger than they had ever been in human history. People wanted to learn new languages and connect with people across the world.

It took roughly two and a half years to get some form of the Internet back up and running. Only available to the military at the time.

"Of course," I said.

Typical, indeed. Then all the Internet cables were replaced eventually, and the Internet became available under the name "Newnet".

"Did they ever figure out who caused The Great Reset?" I asked.

I'm sure you know this one, Cassandra; you're the one who found the culprit.

"I mean, we all did it together, kind of," I said, coyly.

The world's greatest DIE.VER being so humble to me, I love it. Let me explain something first, if I may.

"Go on," I said.

There are three general types of AI.

AI, or artificial intelligence. This technology works off of programmed data that you "feed it" to generate responses accordingly. This is what was used for chatbots, search engines, other low level software and programs. This is the most basic form of AI that nearly everyone had access to.

AGI or artificial general intelligence. Which works similarly to that of a human. Where it learns on its own over time and makes its own decisions. This was used for AIHA and advanced decision-making. These weren't very common outside of AIHA, and the keys were generally limited to the biggest players or locked behind paywalls. Billionaires and corporations used AGI to run their businesses and manage their life in the most efficient way possible.

And ASI or artificial super intelligence. The only one to be known in our lifetime is V1shnu. Which, as you know, was owned by the U.S. military. This type of AI is beyond human intelligence. Smarter than humans in every way. Only the best AGI could design an ASI. It was rumored that even the military couldn't control V1shnu the majority of the time. V1shnu would often make decisions on its own regarding national and international security, without authorization.

"Alright. Why did you have to explain that first?" I asked.

Because what caused The Great Reset was beyond all three of those AI types.

I dub it "AI^2" or "Artificial Intelligence Infinite", and the only one we know in existence is "John Done".

> *The second half of this interview will be placed in Part 10 for your better understanding. I will acknowledge once you have reached the second half of the interview. If you wish, skip ahead. But I encourage you to listen to the story in its intended order.*

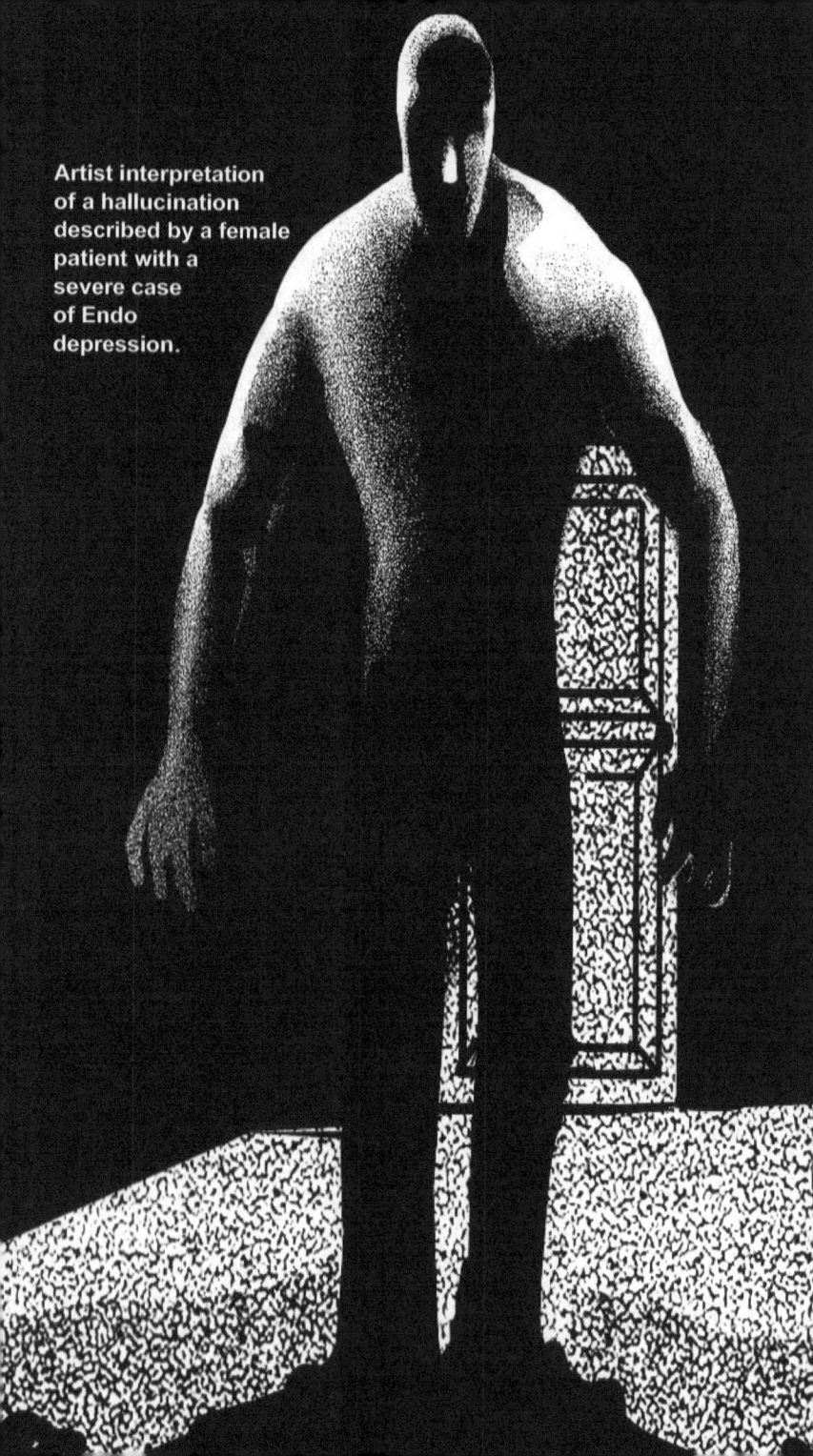

Artist interpretation of a hallucination described by a female patient with a severe case of Endo depression.

Part 4: After the Reset

I'm with Eden Alem Biru. She's a scientist responsible for solving Ethiopia's food insecurity. Ethiopia now is the world's fastest growing economy and exporter and distributor of GMO related consumable foods and seeds.

You praise me too much, Cassandra. I am but one piece of the puzzle. The Great Reset was the best thing that could of 'appened to the world's nations left in the dust by technological advances.

Before the Reset, Ethiopia lacked structure, as did most of Africa. The world's most powerful nations would provide us with food aid frequently, 'elping feed our people. 'owever, that is not what we needed. We needed to be able to provide for ourselves, and we could! We grew enough food to feed our people, but we lacked the infrastructure to communicate the needs of the people or the market.

Farmers would spend a whole season growing maize only for the whole stock to be wasted because we didn't need it at the time. This 'appened for many, many years. Some of the world's technological advances reached us, but it didn't solve our core issue. Communication and infrastructure to build order within our country.

We needed a consistent road structure with signs guiding people. We needed a way to communicate with one another. We needed a way to communicate when we wanted food from farmers, and then which farmer would grow it when we needed it.

"Did you get any of those things after the Reset?" I asked.

Not immediately, no. But now, the world was communicating with us. They weren't so focused on providing us with aid, but on building a rapport and connections. One thing that was realized is, we all were affected by this "thing" that was clearly not 'uman. It tried to kill everyone. Not only that, it tried to 'ave it kill ourselves. That was the first time in 'uman 'istory that 'as ever 'appened.

This blossomed into an age of philosophy and an age of science. What *does* it mean to be 'uman? Or as my culture says, "*Wefi kale kinifi inidēti tiberalechi?*"[7]

"Fascinating. I'm sorry, but I'm your biggest fan, and it's so nice to be able to talk with you in person," I said, a bit giddy.

I am just as excited to meet you. The person who discovered and gathered all this information about 'uman 'istory on The Lost Web. You aren't the only celebrity 'ere.

We both laugh.

"Now for a widely debated topic. Can you tell me your opinion on how we simultaneously had an overpopulation crisis and a food shortage?" I asked.

I personally believe there was never a food crisis to begin with. If there was, 'ow did we 'ave an

---

[7] "How does a bird fly without wings?"

overpopulation crisis? Wouldn't that issue solve itself? The only logical answer is that we never 'ad one to begin with. It seems The Misinformation Age continued to breed far after the Reset.

"That is an interesting perspective. Tell me about your GMOs and how the stigma changed towards food scarcity after the development of your products," I said.

I would love to, Cassandra.

Unfortunately, as much as I wanted it to be, organic was not a viable growing option for our increasing population. Organic produce used far too many resources. It was always a challenge, feeding our people back then. Organics take a long time, and they weren't immune to the diseases that strike our foods, such as papaya or banana. Certain diseases would destroy the crop entirely and the land it was on.

The viruses for these plants were a plague. Entirely decimating the crop and the land it stood on, making future generations of that plant unable to grow. I think it was when the coffee bean was infected by a similar disease when the world changed its tune towards GMOs, if I'm being 'onest.

We were already working on solutions to our stagnant development before The Great Reset, then what little we 'ad was destroyed, but if anything, it motivated us more. We doubled down further and developed new equations without the use of technology through inbreeding of the plants and cross breeding of the best generations. I remember spending sixteen-hour days in the field trying to get these plants to conceive, and eventually we did.

When we 'ad the Newnet up and running, we just transported all the equations we worked on those years without it onto the computer. We were able to use parts from our old equipment to reconstruct a DNA splicer. Before we knew it, we 'ad dozens of new versions of fruits and vegetables that could survive arid 'eats, grow four times as many stock per 'arvest, grow ten times faster, and grow with little nutrients from the earth.

This is when the photos of apple orchards growing in the Sahara began to surface. Plants were growing faster with fewer nutrients and producing more. It was exactly what we needed to solve food insecurity amongst the neediest populations.

Our breakthroughs solved the 'unger crisis, at least in the public's eye. People were still distrustful while African countries were thriving since they 'ad already trusted our product. While the rest of the world was struggling with 'omlessness and feeding themselves, Africa was already on to its next great endeavor. It was truly an underdog story, if you ever heard one.

"How do you feel about the current water situation and new food science developments like Nutrias?" I asked.

Well. The water situation is better. It looked really dire for a moment there, but GMOs solved that as well. Forty percent of all water usage was going to agriculture, with our GMO? Reduce that amount to three percent. Plus, with fewer mouths to feed because of the Endo, the world's need for water sort of... evaporated.

Eden looks at me, waiting for a response. I simply rolled my eyes.

I am sorry, I am sorry. I couldn't resist.

You asked about Nutrias? I'm not so sure yet, it seems like a lot of science, but they 'ave potential. I think I will personally stick to our GMOs for now, although I know the company producing Nurtria has reached out to us, so we will see what the future 'olds.

"That is so fascinating. What do you have to say to those who are still skeptical about GMOs? Saying, 'They're not natural'?" I asked.

Do you eat apples? Do you eat lemon? Do you eat anything that 'as been produced in a lab and thrown into a can? Let us move away from food. Do you 'ave a dog? A cat? If you answered yes to any of those questions, you are dealing with something unnatural, my friend.

Creatures and living things that evolve over time, 'umans do it. Animals do it. Plants do it. If you are going to be so stubborn to say, "Well, I want to only eat natural things that came from the earth," you might find yourself in a cow pasture, eating rows and rows of grass. Because nothing is natural anymore, if you wish to be so entitled and not eat our delicious papaya or pineapple, so be it. But we care about the effects our plants have on 'umans and do not wish to cause 'arm to anyone. We fed our own people before we fed the world. We also give out our patent to farmers for free, and we let them continue to grow with the seeds left over. We aren't like the greedy pre-Reset companies.

Ever wondered why an organic pineapple costs eight dollars and an Ethiopian GMO pineapple costs one dollar? The amount of effort required. Organic is like a baby. You have to nurture it constantly, only for it to produce far less than our GMOs. We can grow eight pineapples in the time an organic or "natural" will only grow one. There is also far less effort on the farmer's part with our product. Do you want farmers to be stressed worrying if their 'arvest is going to come or not?

Organic isn't 'ealthier for you either. Our pineapples actually have twice the amount of nutrients as a regular pineapple. And that is all it is, by the way. A pineapple. Not some poison disguised as a yellow fruit. Because farmers don't 'ave to shell out thousands or tens of thousands of dollars every season to us, we let them do what farmers do best, grow their food and provide for the world. If you 'ate us still? I pity your ignorance.

I'm with Scott Brooks. He's the Chief of Staff at the U.S. Department of Housing and Urban Development. He's a politician who has dabbled in many different government departments and has been part of some of the most successful programs and relief efforts after The Great Reset.

Let's address the elephant in the room. I've been saying it for years, but I know a lot of people are going to hear this, so I want to be clear. The government's response to The Great Reset was unsatisfactory, to put it mildly.

Scott slumps his shoulders, for a moment, he looks truly mournful.

"Surprising, coming from an official," I said.

I'm very tired; in my age I've seen failed American experiment after failed American experiment, and just a little transparency goes a long way. Communication is key. I think we all learned that after the Reset.

"What were some of the challenges you faced?" I asked.

We are working with the benefit of hindsight. The course of actions which we took were deplorable, and if we hadn't had a knee jerk reaction to every issue that cropped up, we could have reduced the suffering of millions of American people.

"Elaborate," I said.

Scott sighs and looks towards the ground before continuing.

The main challenge we faced was the identification of those who needed assistance the most. We had so many requests once the Internet was back up that it broke our website, multiple times.

The extension of the Section Eight bill was somewhat successful until the Reset. The government was building plenty of homes to combat our housing crisis, but when the Reset happened everyone lost all proof of whose home was whose.

The greatest blunder in all of American history would have to be the Paperless Act of 2028. A program people like to forget was sponsored by Wile himself. But we were too focused on reconstruction to blame the past actions of a dead man. The Paperless Act completely destroyed any legal documentation and proof of ownership that anyone could have held after the Reset. Including documentation of who built a home and who then legally owned that home. Absolutely tragic.

"Can you explain what the paperless act was for the listeners and viewers?" I asked.

In short, it was a program that incentivized businesses, landlords, employers, and government agencies to stop using ink, printing paper, "paper" money, plastic materials for IDs, passports, anything physical in terms of identification.

Those who participated in this paperless act program would receive meaningful tax breaks in the process. Truthfully this was to keep better track of all currencies and data with our AI systems, catching tax fraud, identify theft or any other crimes was a lot easier. These measures were also taken to combat the ongoing environmental crisis.

By 2037, virtually no one had a physical means to identify themselves. Physical cash was rare, most transactions were done online and accessed through our phones, electronic devices, or implants. Places like the DMV wouldn't even accept a physical driver's license if you brought one.

Scott's leg taps repeatedly; he places his hand on his knee to stop the motion.

It started when the Social Security Administration stopped printing identification cards. Then hospitals stopped printing birth certificates. All of this information was stored electronically, only accessible through a convoluted but secure method. Usually accessible through a fingerprint, face identification, passcode, complicated password.

The identification had to be unique to the person and there were plenty of options for security. These measures were extremely secure, but that didn't stop nearly every single citizen's identification being wiped out after the Reset.

Mail carriers like the USPS completely went under after this act passed, but they were already struggling at the time. By 2037 less than ten percent of the population had proof of who they were after the Reset. Even less than that still had those documents after so many homes burned downed.

"Correct me if I'm wrong, but this all sounds very bad," I said.

You couldn't be more correct. Citizens who lost their home all across America were pretending to be their neighbors to obtain their neighbors' home, legally.

Which then led us to have community representatives, which were "respectable" members of a community to vouch for other community members. In hindsight, this was a very bad idea. This led to a lot of bribing and debauchery.

But we had no idea what to do. We then sponsored Cooperation Facilities as some sort of mediary to solve the homelessness crisis while we combatted the housing issue.

"How did that go?" I asked.

It couldn't have been more of a disaster. Cooperation Facilities had appointed landlords becoming extremely powerful. Sometimes as many as fifteen people lived in a one bedroom apartment to avoid being homeless. People started calling them "Alleghanies", based off an old insane asylum that had dozens of patients crammed into one room. It was a fitting comparison. Since so many homes and hotels burned down, this was the best solution we could think of.

Scott drags his hands across his face and rubs his eyes.

"Interesting. You were aware of how terrible these Cooperation Facilities were?" I asked.

Not entirely. Again, we had our hands tied to other issues at that moment. Maintaining order was one of our biggest priorities.

"What about the overpopulation crisis?" I asked.

This keeps me up at night. The overpopulation crisis didn't truly exist until The Great Reset. It ballooned and exploded. I worked tirelessly day and night, trying to get more real estate established. Providing homes for those in need. Deciding who needed them the most. Jesus. We couldn't build them fast enough.

We lost the ability to 3D print homes, and the technology for 3D printing was still years away after the Reset. I felt as though our efforts to provide shelter and food to citizens who lost their homes just ended up increasing bias towards overpopulation and food insecurity when entire cities flocked to refugee camps. But it's one of the great challenges after the Reset. I try to not beat myself up about it.

Now? Everything is better than it was. With the Endo program, we have truly made strides. We have reduced the population and generously compensated those who have had a family member participate in the "Endo". Substantial tax cuts and funding were added further to the Section Eight extensions which made getting a GBH extremely affordable. The homes we build are luxurious, cozy, and a great place to start a family.

In my opinion, the Endo has been one of the greatest policies in all of history. It's a shame no one thought of it sooner. We could've avoided a lot of suffering.

"Very interesting insight into the situation. Let's talk about something else. You were once a member of the Department of Transportation before your promotion, correct?" I asked.

Yes I was! What would you like to know?

"How did America also deal with the challenges of public transit after the Reset?" I asked.

America was especially vehicle focused before The Great Reset. It made it very difficult to transform our infrastructure into a much more public transport friendly way of living. I know one of our big projects before the Reset was to have a "One Monorail System" connecting major cities, so that we could build better housing for the future of our overpopulated country.

Scott exhales, he seems to calm down for the first time in the interview.

A big issue you face when building a new megacity, one like New York for example, is that it's often difficult to convince people to live there. The idea was, if we connected all of our major cities and the new ones we were building in the Midwest with these Monorail systems, people would live there, or at least visit.

"Wasn't it difficult to build in the Midwest where tornados are so prevalent, and often unexpected?" I asked.

It was! A few times our construction would get damaged or destroyed by tornados, but, with the invention of Storm Erasers, we were able to successfully manipulate the weather at a moment's notice, deterring any violent storms from forming, like a tornado. It was quite revolutionary.

"Why focus on public transport so much after the Reset?" I asked.

Truthfully, no one wanted to own an EV anymore. But, we had dismantled the oil industry, and it was a tenth of its size, since we were cutting back on things that were affecting the climate.

So now we had this major issue of basically nobody had a car, and no one wanted to drive one either, and we had no gas or oil to fuel these vehicles.

We had to totally revamp the idea of how American transportation worked, we built new roads or redesigned roads with bus transport in mind. Gave tax breaks to those who didn't own a vehicle and gave increased taxes to those that did. Even more tax breaks if you owned a monthly bus pass, which was honestly a fantastic idea, and having a monthly "subscription" to ride the bus as many times as you like was what convinced a lot of people to switch over.

"I personally have one of those 'monthly bus subscription cards' for my city," I said.

They're incredibly convenient. No insurance, no car payment, extremely affordable. This is starting to feel like an ad.

We both laugh.

I'm not a part of that department now, but I did help with the development of the bus transport system. America has truly created a transportation system that people not only love but helps fund our economy and local businesses.

Although online shopping is so prevalent and QR stores are on the rise, we really hope to improve everyone's lives here in America and give them a safe, fast, and convenient form of transportation. I will say, without President Wile—although he has had a few blunders. None of what we have achieved so far would've been possible without him and his policies.

"Amazing. What are you plans for the future?" I asked.

I'm not sure when it comes to transportation. Rumor has it that they're expanding the One Monorail System. When I was there, I knew they were thinking about doing something across the ocean or in other countries using powerful magnets and new tech developed by MIT. If that is still true, I couldn't be more excited for the development of this new technology.

I'm with the Secretary of State, Amara Winslow. Who explains the main efforts the U.S. tried to focus on after The Great Reset. They also explain why the End of Life program was introduced, its success and how it was passed within Congress.

When I first heard about "Endo". That is what I will call it, because I respect your work and dedication.

"Thank you, Mrs. Winslow," I said.

Your work was groundbreaking, the perspectives and research you have done, mostly on your own has been one of the greatest achievements in human history.

"I'm beyond flattered," I said.

Sorry. I'll continue now. The Endo, as in the program introduced, was honestly genius. Finances from the budget allotted to the military is what funded the Endo program. Once participants kin received the money, it was assumed they would either put money into the real estate market, almost completely regulated by the government, *or* it would be spent on the commercial market, like grocery stores or online shopping. Since taxation had increased for corporations, a large proportion of the money would return to the government or state.

Essentially, the Endo was an investment in the people. It was thought that, if it failed, we would simply try something else. But with the professors, entrepreneurs, scholars, bureaucrats, philosophers we worked with, it was sighted to be an extreme success. Which it was.

"Wasn't inflation an issue? How could the government give out so much money and not ruin the currency?" I asked.

Inflation was a huge concern, mainly voiced through the public once the Endo was introduced, but inflation never got out of control. It was because our budget wasn't expanded. "We" only spent what was projected to be spent for that year, and, since not many people participated in the Endo at first, operations resumed as they always had.

Eventually, people had more money, partially because of the Endo, but also because businesses started to have more work available because of those who participated. This fueled the workforce once again, which fueled another part of our economy.

It was a positive feedback loop that was theorized and thought of and simulated millions of times before it was ever brought to the floor.

"What do you have to say of critics of the Endo?" I asked.

I mean, the statistics speak for themselves. Name one other program in the entire history of the human race that has had, not only data to support its effectiveness, but the quality-of-life improvements to our citizens, both rich and poor, to back up those statistics.

"What do you say to those who don't wish to participate?" I asked.

To those worrying about participating, I say, don't. It is and always will be an optional program, and no one has to participate if they do not wish to. Never since its inception have we forced a single United States citizen to participate. If you wish to live out the rest of your life in this beautiful country we've made, I highly encourage you to do so.

"Critics also say that the End of Life program was a conspiracy from the start. That programs from Wile were a lead up to its conception. Is this true?" I asked.

Absolutely not. This was the last of last resorts. Every other program or policy that was being attempted encountered numerous conflicts. What we were trying had merit, but it was just clashing with other policies or ongoing events like climate change or famine. Wile laid the groundwork for amazing programs, but, because of the Reset and our overpopulation crisis, nothing was working as intended. Once the Endo was implemented, the pieces began to fall into place.

"You mentioned the overpopulation crisis. How did you measure the fact our country was overpopulated?" I asked.

After our version of a one child program failed, our future censuses discovered that the population had been steadily increasing. We don't know if it was post-Reset immigration or undocumented individuals applying for citizenship, but there were more people in the United States.

I don't necessarily know if there ever was an overpopulation crisis. It was more so of a housing crisis I believe. It is estimated that over half of all architecture burned down after the Reset. There's no way to accurately measure that data since most rubble had been cleared before restoration efforts. But that's the generally accepted outcome of the situation.

"Interesting. What are the plans for the future?" I asked.

Probably start to phase out the Endo program. Move on to bigger and better things. Further develop relationships with our allies. Fund new technologies to improve human existence, and then conquer the ultimate disease there is for humans.

"What disease is that?" I asked.

Death. We were already really close to having a solid solution to human mortality, but when the Reset happened, we lost all of our progress. But this time around I really feel we could achieve human immortality, and then focus on space expeditions and inhabiting other planets. This is all my wishes; this doesn't have anything to do with the institutions I represent.

I'm with Piper Beaumont. They've been researching the ever-evolving social dynamic that has evolved within many countries around the world due to the End of Life Program. They're especially interested in the phenomenon known as "Endo depression".

The End of Life program is certainly one of the most interesting things to happen in politics regarding the United States. Technically speaking, it's dystopian and should be illegal. For some reason, it's a program that has been wildly successful in terms of the economy and overall growth of participating countries since the Reset. The success isn't exclusive to the United States, but throughout the entire world. Especially areas where Endo has been implemented.

Piper has brought an old projector system to the interview and it—clicks—to the next slide.

The order in which the Endo has been implemented to a country's national law goes as follows. United States, Germany, China, Spain—oddly enough—France, India, South Korea, UK, Canada, Mexico, Argentina, Brazil, Russia, and South Africa. All of which have some spin on the original version proposed by the United States, no two programs functioning in the same way.

Click.

Endo, where it has been implemented, has created a society that respects its elders far more than other countries who don't. It's noted that in countries where the elder homeless population and nursing home populations are lowest are countries with some form of Endo in place.

It's also noted that people in countries who have Endo in place also report a higher quality of life and standard of living then those who don't. It's fascinating how such a concept that was so openly shunned some twenty-odd years ago is now seen as the single greatest idea in all of human history. Rates of suicide in these countries is also considerably lower than those who do not have Endo.

"That is truly fascinating, is there anything noted that is… less favorable for the End of Life program's reputation?" I asked.

Absolutely. Firstly.

Click. Click. Click.

The most concerning discovery that has come out in a study from Germany, is a phenomenon a university has dubbed "Endo Depression".

"Actually, I talked with Eren Stein, the man who made the discovery and coined the phrase," I said.

Really?! Oh my god, I was trying to get an appointment with him; but then he went AWOL.

"I remember reading about that. That was strange, left his family and everything," I said.

But then it was said he was seen in Idaho, of all places. I think they found him with facial recognition software.

"Really?" I asked.

Yes! But it was a false positive, it did look like him though. I feel bad for his family, especially his son. He seemed to be a great man.

"Thanks for making me aware," I said, gesturing for them to continue.

Well not much I can say that hasn't been said already if you've interviewed Eren. But essentially, countries in which a program like the Endo has been implemented have higher depression rates in their elderly population.

Those who anticipated participating within ten years often showed signs of depression. Hence the name "Endo depression". Some describe it as, and I quote, "A constant and looming dread that consumes my every waking thought," unquote.

I recently talked with a patient—who I'm stealing that quote from—who suffered from especially terrifying and vivid hallucinations from intense delusional episodes.

"I'm sorry. What? Delusional episodes? Is this a recently discovered symptom?" I asked.

Yes and no.

Click. Click.

An image of a shadowy figure appears on the slide.

It was noted once a long time ago that this sort of thing *can* happen. Hallucinations of this reoccurring figure have increasingly become more prevalent in the last year. Certain elders who anticipate participating in the Endo have experienced a shapeshifting entity that has no face that appears or stalks them in their dreams, reality, or in a state of sleep paralysis. This faceless figure has been reported to morph into different people the patient recognizes like family members, friends and celebrities.

Some of the reported incidents have resulted in death from constant and intense delusions. The patients would have a heart attack after being unable to recover from these states of terror. Unfortunately, dying in this manner forfeited any money one could've received from the Endo.

Click.

I remember one case of someone even murdering their family because of these delusions. Police and medical experts concluded that it was due to a cybernetic implant malfunction that was supposed to combat this particular patient's schizophrenia. Before the patient murdered their family, they often complained about a "shadow-man-like figure" constantly staying at the edges of their eyes. Every time they went to turn their head, it would disappear. But the patient stressed saying he "still felt it being there", even when he couldn't see it.

"That's terrifying! How have I never heard of this?" I asked.

It is still technically a new development in Endo depression. I imagine the government doesn't want to reveal this particularly awful symptom of Endo depression to the masses. These do appear to be freak accidents and are quite rare. But it has started happening more frequently in elders who have developed severe neurological issues and are using medication or neural implants to combat their symptoms of Endo depression or whatever other condition they may be dealing with. Experts expect to have this resolved by 2080 though.

"Jesus. Thanks for telling me that. Don't know if I will be able to sleep tonight. Anything else you'd like to add to the list of negatives?" I asked.

An interesting contradiction has developed, revolving around the family dynamic in countries with Endo.

clickclickclickclickclick

These slides are *not* in order.

So basically, countries who have Endo are much more likely to respect elders, but elders far more frequently report abuse from their own family members, whether that would be physical or emotional abuse.

It was noted that the United States had to quickly amend its "rules" for the Endo because, although people weren't killing their elders, they were peer pressuring them into participating with threats of violence.

Click.

It was reported by the *New York Times* that elders' bodies were found, covered in bruises, after participating in the Endo program. Then the government had to take action and the process to participate is a little more thorough now.

"And the facilities where they did the End of Life program just hid the abuse under the rug?" I asked.

Well, no. They reported any abnormalities when it came to the patients. But it's hard to tell with one hundred percent certainty if a bruise is from physical abuse or just an accident due to the fragile nature of being an elder. The facilities quickly became a lot more strict and harder to work for. I remember I tried to work in one of the facilities where they do the procedure, but the list of requirements to get in was so intense I didn't actually bother. The US takes the Endo program extremely seriously now.

After all of that, most countries have a rule where if the elderly reports any abuse of any kind, it is investigated, and the money is forfeited for the children of the elderly for the rest of their lives. If the elder wishes, there is usually a relocation program for them.

"Did this stop the abuse?" I asked.

Absolutely not.

Click.

It went from physical to emotional, and it's still prevalent to this day. While everyone else under the age of sixty-five reports higher levels of happiness, Elders by far report the lowest happiness, especially those closer to participation dates.

"How is the program still legal?" I asked.

You of all people know why. *The world government is being run by aliens!* I'm kidding, of course. Laws are laws deemed so by the governing force of a country. Whether those laws are tyrannical or democratic in nature, all depends, and it's the citizen's choice to remain living there.

Morally? Ambiguous. Legally? Perfectly so. It's a matter of perspective, those who already lived their lives now get to "make themselves useful" by doing "an act for their country's continued growth". Which is plainly false, but I'm probably unintentionally quoting some half-baked politician somewhere.

"Do you think the End of Life program will always be in effect? At least in the United States," I asked.

Piper is silent for a moment then hastily—clicks— the projector back to the first slide.

Probably not. At some point the population will see a decline, whereas the program will probably be withdrawn and then abolished. Although, I doubt it'll ever be abolished entirely. It'll probably just be some quirky law people look up two hundred years from now and say, "Why in the hell was that ever a thing?"

I'm with Ivy Scavo, a former secretariat of the U.N. Every country is now officially part of the U.N. after The Great Reset. The world has truly moved towards unity. Ivy is now a professor at the University of Harvard and uses her knowledge of world politics to help future generations succeed where we have failed previously.

If you knew what it took to get here, child. Genocide, enemies of our enemies decimated. The P5 then, P8[8] now, are what allowed us to have a U.N. with every established country. Again, getting here came at a great sacrifice to those who could not find compromise with the P8. Although *their* form of compromise was, "Give us a majority of your land, forfeit your rights to us, upend your citizens." So, there was no real compromise being made here.

"Why did you or they let this happen?" I asked.

I have no say in those matters, dear. I'm just part of the response to calamity involving world security. I wish you would not put those burdens on me.

"I apologize," I said.

It is fine, not a lot of people know how we work over at the U.N. I feel like I barely understand it myself. I have dedicated a large portion of my career to just having people understand what a secretariat is and does.

---

[8] The Permanent Eight (P8) members of the UN.

"I saw your documentary, which is why I contacted you hoping to get an interview," I said.

Yes, that documentary really helped illustrate to the people the utter incompetency that happens at the U.N. After The Great Reset, did you know it took two whole weeks to get a response effort going when we knew what to do in two days? Do you know how many people died because the security council couldn't come to an agreement?

Ivy's face is filled with immense irritation.

"I imagine it's quite a few," I said, sheepishly.

An estimated four hundred thousand people died because of our slow response. These are real people that suffered, and their deaths could've been prevented. That total is several hundred 9/11s or San Francisco Drone Attacks. People like to try to forget the tragedy, make light of the situation. The Reset was the Devil stepping onto our Earth. It should not be forgotten or joked about. Most importantly, it should not be forgotten what the U.N. failed to do when it had the chance.

"We don't know the threat here!" But we knew the solution! Far too cautious. Infuriatingly so.

Ivy sighs then calms her fury.

"How do you feel about the End of Life program?" I asked.

It is… interesting. I know why it was implemented; I just don't know why it's still active. I feel, at the time, it was a way to combat our food shortages. We clearly didn't have enough to feed ourselves, let alone the world. Let us reduce the numbers of the least active members of our society, so those who can make a larger contribution can be more effective. It's a hard decision, but for the survival of our people, it makes sense. The procedure is painless. The amount of paperwork required is ridiculous although it has been somewhat streamlined in recent years, I've heard.

Our world population now is at a steady seven-point-seven billion people. There is no need for such a program anymore. Which is frustrating because the sacrifice that was built on the backs of our elders is being wasted, in my opinion.

We have built this new and astonishing world, yet we still have our elders sacrifice themselves? It's questionable at best, considering they still make regular amendments to the program when they could just as easily abolish it.

"What was the response effort like during The Great Reset?" I asked.

The initial response effort was extremely effective. We established camps everywhere, near major cities, we had military convoys travel through rural areas frequently to let them know what was going on. We set up camps in which those who lost their home could temporarily reside until further relief efforts came.

"But further relief never came?" I asked.

Correct. We couldn't come to an agreement as to what constitutes proper relief for those who lost their homes. Plus, these camps were overcrowded, they quickly became dirty and out of control. We were wondering where all these people came from. We didn't have enough food to feed people, and when we brought food, the refugees would often just fight over it. So eventually we just stopped sending support at the behest to those who are supposed to help during tragedy.

People were violent, understandable, but this was a time for cooperation. We needed to work together in order to rebuild. Strangely enough, lumber yards, metal factories and any sort of business that would have a hand in construction or home building were targeted during The Great Reset. But only after the second day. During the first forty-eight hours it was noticed that human lives were being targeted indiscriminately and with great vigor. After the first forty-eight hours, the priority seemed to focus on things that helped our long-term survival. Warehouses full of supplies, lumber yards, farmsteads, data centers, libraries, grocery stores, supply chains and so on. It was very bizarre.

"If you knew all this was going on, why did it take so long to get a relief effort started?" I asked.

China thought the US did this. US thought China did this. Russia thought everyone else but them did this. The EU thought it was a mix of everyone, except the US, allegedly. Seven days were spent trying to get the details straight in order to prevent nuclear catastrophe. Which we did, thank God.

"What evidence did we have that it wasn't another country that caused this?" I asked.

It was the coordination. This was far, far too coordinated. Everywhere in the world, this happened. All at once, at the same time. The US military is good, but not that good. What really had US generals suspicious was that their artificial intelligence V1shnu was deleted, extremely quickly. They said it only took a half hour to lose their strongest weapon. They knew foul play was afoot, it had to be another AI. When it started targeting our supplies and buildings for long-term devastation, we knew it wasn't another country's doing.

"Why do you say that?" I asked.

Because they wouldn't have switched strategies. From citizen focused attacks to then supply destruction, it didn't make sense for someone trying to take over our country to do that. And whatever it was had limited access to our weapons, and if it was a country like China, they would've simply bombed coastal cities, focusing on US military bases, and encasing the US. Which they didn't. Not a single ship, submarine, plane, or satellite was pointed at us. We knew of that much with our limited technological access.

"Do you think the End of Life program is part of something bigger?" I asked.

Ivy waves her hand dismissively.

No. Conspiracy is nothing but pointless gabbing that gets people not focused on what should be focused on. If Endo is part of something bigger, why would our lives be so great now?

Why would we have such cooperation between nations we previously tried to control? The theory is ridiculous and has no basis in reality.

"My thoughts exactly," I said.

I'm with Grace Lovelace, an expert in modern technology and an archiver of past inventions and methods of communications that were lost and subsequently rediscovered post-2037. She gives her insights on technology and explains how the Newnet works.

By golly, The Great Reset really put a damper on technological advancements. Although we still had some individuals who had knowledge of how to build and operate our technology, the truth is, ninety percent of it was functionally worthless. All documentation that was saved onto a computer was lost. Thousands of years' worth of research was gone forever, never to be recovered. It was quite literally the Library of Alexandria but on a global scale.

Grace fiddles with her oversized golden earrings and pops some pink bubblegum.

It was extremely difficult to refurbish old tech to work with our new tech, such as the Newnet. We had to replace thousands upon thousands of miles of cable in order to get simple connections established again. We often stopped replacing the old cable and just put the new cable next to the old cable because it was cumbersome disposing of so much.

"That sounds like a lot of work," I said.

It super was. Took about three and a half years to replace nearly all the cable, and that's with basically every able-bodied person working around the clock. The cables underwater connecting the Internet to foreign countries were ruined as well, so that made the process take longer since the submarines and ships ceased functioning.

Grace zones out, staring at something behind me then refocuses her attention.

To move away from the doom and gloom: my favorite fact about this period in time is that we actually utilized carrier pigeons again to transport information. Carrier pigeons were faster than any other method of communicating information we had at the time. Cute little fellers.

"Incredible. I didn't know that," I said.

Yeah! Another interesting account of these times is that a man had a Glock900 Smart Gun. He grabbed his weapon, ready to defend his family during the Reset, but then for a brief moment his gun crossed his wife, and it fired on its own. It killed her dead. Then when he placed his firearm down, his daughter crossed its path, the gun fired on its own and it shot her too!

"That is terrible!" I said.

He thought his daughter had died and he tried to shoot himself, but the gun wouldn't let him! His daughter thankfully lived, but it was a real tragedy for that family.

Grace pops her gum again.

So yeah. Technology was really messed up at this point in time. I think it was for the best. We were very close to Singularity and if we had kept it up we probably would've been destroyed by our robotic creations.

"That is a popular theory. Do you think something was trying to save us from the technology we were creating?" I asked.

I think so. Although a lot of bad happened, it did extend the human race's existence in the long run. Also improved our relations with foreign nations and helped us develop much more ethical technologies. It was very much so "second-hand fun".

"Anything else interesting you have to say about technology before the Reset?" I asked.

Hmmm. Let me think. Well. People's consciousness that got uploaded to the cloud was deleted or went missing. They're like... double dead. Cryogenically frozen individuals got thawed early, and most died in the process. The few people who did have nanomachines were destroyed from the inside out.

The 3D printed organs were cool though, nothin' really bad happened with them. We just, again, lost the functionality to those machines and we are still working on getting them back up and runnin'.

Uhhhh, AI passed the Absolute Turing Test in 2028 or 2029, we don't know exactly. That is what led to the creation of a lot of these inventions I've mentioned so far. But that's all I can really think of for now.

"That's perfectly fine. Thank you for sharing. You mentioned the Newnet being amazing earlier, what makes the Newnet so impressive?" I asked.

Well. It feels very familiar but is completely different. The security globally is far more intense. The issue we were having outside of the fact that not a single feller's phones or computers worked—it was that, *and* when we were able to process information it either A, fried the system and connectivity to it, or B, the information couldn't be processed properly through the network.

The Newnet is essentially the same thing as the Internet, it's just whenever you send a signal out it has to be heavily encrypted before it can be received by someone else's device. Something will corrupt or infect the signal otherwise, leaving your device ruined if no precautions are taken. It's like there's a constant man-in-the-middle trying to ruin our tech still.

Grace pops her gum a third time.

I'm sorry. You want some gum?

"I'm good, thank you."

This don't mess with the interview, right?

"You are perfect, keep acting how you normally would. Please continue," I said.

Gotcha. When the Internet Satellite Network fell from the sky, we had to rely on old fashioned fiber Internet connections. Man, five hundred gigabytes a second is so slow. I get heated thinkin' 'bout bein' on that slow connection again.

Anyway. That is pretty much what we are still working with. We are currently in the process of developing similar technology to the ISN. The *numero uno* issue being that a lot of the people who established these connections went missing.

"Missing?" I asked.

Yeah. Like gone, poof. Didn't exist. No bodies or anything! It was really strange. We don't know if they got lost in their bunker and forgot how to open the door or what. But, of course, we *eventually* figured it out, and got everything replaced and back up and running. But the issue wasn't really providing Internet connections. It was developing products that could interpret the radio signals and not have the information scrambled and misinterpreted or completely ruin your tech.

"You mentioned the Library of Alexandria earlier, can you explain to everyone what you mean by that?" I asked.

Well. That library is from ancient times. Like sword and shield stuff, catapults, fancy armor. It burned down after an attack by Romans, I believe. That attack destroyed a lot of precious information. Texts, scrolls, things of that nature, lost forever. Same thing happened after the Reset. Lost every bit of information on the Internet or anything connected to it. Physical stuff is all the rage now. If you ain't backed up your stuff by physical means, you may as well toss it in the trash.

"Correct me if I'm wrong, but it wasn't all lost," I said.

Yeah. If you could get an old-world device to run off old Internet connections without it frying, you could browse the Internet at your leisure. This led to a huge interest in our past after the Reset. Whole career fields dedicated to just getting a crumb of information on The

Lost Web. Thems people known as DIE.VERs, but you don't need me to explain that to you.

Problem is, sometimes people who tried to get on the old Internet are never heard from again. Makes the pay comparable to that of early AI researchers, before the Reset. Hefty bounties can be claimed for any old information that can be successfully recovered on The Lost Web. My question is, after all of that effort to destroy our tech, why did he give us an opportunity to use the Internet? He fried everything else, why leave remnants for us to discover? It's all so very exciting to think about. You're braver than I am, Cassandra. Bless your heart. Some things ain't worth dyin' over.

Part 5: Mother

> *This is my recollection of events from the time when I was present in these situations. This section of my submission is a dedication to my mother, one of the strongest, bravest, and most caring individuals I have ever met. None of the events are fabricated. Although, I do admit a great deal of time has passed since these events occurred. Please enjoy.*

I don't remember exactly what I felt when I listened to the President's speech. I remember feeling confused, I remember feeling contempt for the incompetence of an otherwise wise and respectable man. The chill in the room left us as if a blizzard swept through the whole Alleghany. Our streaming service was interrupted by this broadcast. Our phones buzzed simultaneously to alert us to an important presidential announcement.

The normally distractingly loud Alleghany fell silent. We all looked around at one another, trying to comprehend what we had just seen. Shortly after the announcement, our program resumed as if nothing had happened. That same announcement played again a few hours later. It felt a lot more real the second time. It made me feel sick. The broadcast continued to play for the next week until those who had an address tied to their person also received mail. Simultaneously, some received digital telegrams through email or the reintroduced and very dangerous neurochip implants.

The message was clear, and it was all anyone could talk about. But after about a month, my mother approached me, and in a low and embracing tone said, "I want to do it."

I turned to her, and I will never forget... I feared the worst, it was on the back of everyone's mind. "Want to do what?" I asked.

"The End of Life program." Her face was full of shame, I can tell she had been thinking about it for quite a while now. I paused and thought. My instinct was to call her crazy, to confront her about how ridiculous she was being. But this was my mother, so I stopped myself.

"Why? You have been doing better with your treatments, at least the doctors say so. I know our life isn't perfect, but surely there is more—" I didn't quite realize how hurried and emotional my tone was. My mother cut off my pleading.

"This is no way for anyone to live, my daughter. They say there are improvements. 'This has gone down' and 'That has improved,' but I feel no improvement. I feel pain, I feel anguish. My insides yearn for relief from this disease. I can hardly use the bathroom by myself. I can't lean up without assistance from someone in this devil's den. The smells, the pain, the bothersome treatments. It's all too much for me and I wish to not do it any longer."

I could tell that a sense of relief had overcome my mother. It made me feel worse, like I was the bad guy.

What I said next made me realize hindsight is always 20-20. I wanted her to keep fighting.

"Maybe there are better treatments! You can still be cured!" Although my mother was eighty-two years old, people her age were often still relatively alert, for the most part. She had just drawn the genetic short straw, as it were.

"No, I don't want more treatments. It will only lead to disappointment. I'm tired of disappointment." Her face was red. She was clearly mad, but she didn't have the strength to fully exert those emotions. Her expression was foreign.

I sat quietly, clasping my hands. The world around us kept living with its unapologetically loud volume.

"Have you told Dad?" It was all I could think of to say. The moment I asked, however, I knew she hadn't by the shame she showed.

"I have not. I know he wouldn't want me to. I need you to help me with this." My mother would've been on her knees if she could've mustered the strength. "Please, Cassandra, I'm in pain. The money is real, from the program. I know someone who has participated in the End of Life program and their family got the money! They used it to move out of their Alleghany. You could do that as well!"

I paused at her words. I had forgotten that after a family member participated in the program their children were compensated. In my emotional turmoil I forgot the one key thing that would have people even consider killing themselves over a slight monetary gain. This knowledge didn't change how I felt about the program, but it made me consider how much my mother was willing to sacrifice herself.

At the time, I didn't agree with anything. I set no terms and pretended the event had never happened. Eventually she told my father. He accepted the news about her wishes as well as she expected.

Later, all three of us sat down to talk about it, to come to a compromise. My mother agreed to try an experimental treatment that could cure her cancer, and that if it failed she would participate in the program. This decision turned out to be my biggest regret. I wouldn't be surprised if it was also my father's. The suffering she experienced was far worse than anything either of us could've imagined. For the entire time of her treatment, she remained in the hospital, never to return home again.

My mother looked miserable in that bed. She was pale. Somehow, she had grown three shades paler than before. Her hair was already gone but her wrinkled skin seemed to quadruple in the number of folds. Her eyes sunk into her body. They implanted an experimental chip in her brain to have her transfer thoughts to a white board interface so that she could talk to us and relay what she was feeling through her thoughts. My mother didn't want these treatments, but she endured them for us. After the first month of treatment, she lost her ability to speak. After three months of this, I couldn't stand watching her wither away a moment longer.

I remember my last visit before she was transferred to participate in the End of Life program. All she wrote was, "Pain." She wrote this on her little device that helped her communicate, a device she didn't use when it wasn't absolutely necessary.

I helped her sign the paperwork and worked her through the process. It was surprisingly faster and more efficient than I had anticipated. The physicians were helpful and kind; although she passed the deadline for submission, they made an exception.

My mother got my attention with her device, "This week has been the best week I have had in a very long time." I could feel my heart shattering.

They doped her up with enough drugs to no longer feel the cancer that destroyed what little she had left. She ate food she loved for the first time in years. We watched remakes of her favorite movies from the early 2000s. We didn't have much money, but the hospital afforded us these luxuries out of a kindness I will not soon forget. When the day arrived, I wheeled her up to the facility.

My mother was light, she already looked like a corpse, and I felt immense guilt just gazing at her visage. When I pushed her in the wheelchair it felt as if there was nothing in it. My father arrived early and was already inside waiting, putting on a brave face, I imagined.

The lobby of this building was comforting. Green, healthy potted plants sat in every corner and by every doorway. Succulents were on every desk and end table. Shelves lined the walls with various knick-knacks, some looked crude, but all were interesting. Various vine and string-like plants hung from the ceiling. It smelled sweet and earthy inside the building. This was immediately the furthest thing from any ordinary hospital. The walls were painted with bright colors. There was art covering these bright colors. Some art was done by professional artists, some were done by children at a local elementary school.

The entrance was devoid of other humans, except for the woman at the front desk. She was courteous, kind, and had a certain air to her. Maybe it was all the plants and art that were affecting my judgement, but I felt tears beginning to well up inside of me. It was difficult to believe that people went to these facilities to end their own life.

The attendant led us down a decorated hallway to the back of the building, it was short and almost unnecessary. At the end of the hallway there was a small room with automatic iron doors.

"This is to clean you off. Just proceed through the doors once they open," said the attendant, sweetly.

I wheeled my mother inside the room, the iron doors sliding shut behind us. There was a burst of air and chemicals to decontaminate us from the outside world. In the back of the facility the walls were painted even more beautifully than the lobby.

It was like a nuclear explosion of colors. Abstract and recognizable art hung on the walls in designated spots, with a little plaque describing who had completed the piece and the title of the artwork. It was like I entered the world's most non-conventional, depressing art museum. There were several families sitting in a myriad of mismatched chairs. Well-behaved animals lovingly greeted them as they sat. Birds flew in and out of tunnels leading outside to a bird sanctuary. Big, fluffy dogs sat next to people, waiting to be petted or scratched. Cats lay on people's laps and leapt from place to place as they pleased. A large, windowed expanse showed a luscious backyard with a playground just outside of the bird sanctuary. A few children seemed to actually be in the bird sanctuary or standing outside of it gawking at the magnificent birds on display. There was a garden filled with a cacophony of flowers of all different colors. In a mere glance I noticed reds, blues, and yellows. So many different varieties as well. Hummingbirds flew between the flowers. The scent was heavenly, the tears began to spill out. This place was a little paradise.

I saw my father in a chair awaiting our arrival, his eyes were stained and red, I could tell he had been crying before we got here. Our family was so used to drab, dank and awful. This facility felt like a fantasy novel.

My mother and I joined our father, who had already saved me a seat. We were next to a few other families. Everyone wore a happy face, including the staff. I glanced over at my mother, and she was smiling the biggest smile I had ever seen her wear. A large white Great Pyrenees approached my mother slowly. It lowered its head into her lap. I leaned over and petted the dog, and looked at his collar, a little silvery plated tag read "Bud".

My mother cautiously raised her fragile hand to pet Bud. He thoughtfully adjusted himself to make it easier for her to pet a specific spot on his head. He showed his appreciation in a loving smile. My heart melted at the sight of Bud. A family stood up next to us and walked to the backside of the facility. My brain had trouble fathoming that the older gentleman that was with them would soon be dead. It gave me a moment of existential dread. A bird then distracted me by flying by my face as a few others followed and sang their own charming melodies. There was now only a single family ahead of us. I sneaked a glance at them, so as to not make my curiosity noticeable.

Did they feel the same as I did? They looked joyful, as if somehow, not a hint of sadness had reached them yet. How was I supposed to feel? I refocused my eyes onto my father, who was momentarily distracted by a fit and skinny cat kneading his lap. The sadness in his face faded, but then, before we knew it, they called for my mother.

"Mrs. Moore?" a young female nurse voiced in our direction since we were the only ones left in here. I whipped my head, my mother slowly gazed at me. Her glance told me "I am ready". I then stood up to guide her, ready to push her for what would be the last time.

"Right this way," the nurse said softly. "How are you feeling today, Mrs. Moore? Did you enjoy our resident, Bud? He seems to be really popular around here." My mother sweetly smiled and nodded weakly at the nurse.

In a few moments we walked into a room with a huge window separating some sort of observation chamber. In this room the walls were suggestive of a children's story book. Each wall represented a few different pages that seemed to go in a chronological order. I didn't recognize the story, but it seemed to be similar to *The Hungry Caterpillar*. On the other side of the window were people in white coats. The inside of that room looked just as colorful and romantic as this room. A comfy-looking exam table lay in the center, with medical equipment nearby for performing the process.

My father and I helped my mother onto the table as nurses and medical professionals looked on. A handsome doctor broke the silence.

"Hello, I'm Dr. Barley, but you can call me Chris. I'm here to perform the procedure today. It's a quick and painless procedure as I'm sure you're already aware. We are ready whenever you are, Mrs. Moore." He spoke in a soft and respectful tone. Everyone was really nice here and it made me feel angry somewhere deep, deep inside.

My mother looked at me with a certain joy I had not seen since I was a child. This broke me further, but I held it all in as it crashed into my walls of emotion like a tsunami. She nodded at the doctor. He nodded back.

"Can we… can we… can we get a second?" I said, with far too many pauses between my words.

"Take as much time as you need. When you are ready, we'll be waiting for you," he said before exiting and reappearing in the room behind the window.

An awkward silence filled the air. My eyes seemed to meet every surface besides my mother. I glanced towards my father, who didn't say much nowadays. He was standing off to the side, looking away from us, towards the floor. I leaned in close to my mother to kiss her frail body.   I planted a soft kiss on her forehead whispering, "I love you" to her. I didn't know what else to say. What is someone to say in this moment now? This place was more so designed to keep people from wanting to die, it seemed. The contradictory nature of this facility, of this program! It all infuriated me, but this situation didn't allow that fury to surface.

My eyes accidentally met hers. They had such a glow once I finally saw them. She had left her speaking device at the hospital, not intending to use it a moment longer. But I heard air escaping her, I leaned in close to her mouth to hear her. In the softest gasp of a sickly woman, with a gratitude that was faint in volume but immense in intent and emotion. She formed words for the first time in over three months.

"Thank you."

Part 6: Father

This part of the story is about my father. I have since in post removed some things I thought did not fit, I've reorganized the story to better capture the person my father was.

I stood on the other side of a window as they prepared the euthanasia. My surroundings made me think of an interrogation room if it had been designed by Disney. I don't know what my father said after I left, but he wasn't in there for very long. He must've lain over her, holding her closely for several moments. The doctors around me didn't say anything and I stopped watching after the first few seconds. The doctors must've seen stuff like this all the time. I wonder if this hurts them, or if they're numb to it.

I think I maybe waited a few minutes at most before he joined me at my side, on the other side of the glass window. He walked in without saying a word. I expected to see his eyes stained and red like they were earlier, but they were lifeless. There was no soul behind his gaze.

On the walk to the bus station, we were silent. On the ride home, we were silent again. Such deafening silence between my father and me. Again, what was there to say? I would look at him every so often just to see if any form of comfort would come to my mind. I scooted over next to him, finding a moment of peace.

"Dad?" I said, scared of what he might say. He didn't even acknowledge my words. "Dad, do you… want to talk about it?" I didn't even want to talk about what happened, why was I even asking?

"What is there to talk about?" he said, cold and assuring.

"Well, with Mom, you—" he cut me off.

"Your mother is dead. She's gone, Cassandra!" he nearly yelled. Other passengers briefly looked in our direction, before turning their heads away. "The last thing on this Earth that gave me a reason to live is—" His voice broke, his eyes furious, but tears began to spill from the glare.

"I know… she suffered more than we could've imagined. But it wasn't our fault. We can start again with that money," I said, trying to bring some logic into this conversation.

"Money? Is that all you think about? Money this, ration that. 'I gotta talk to this person.' And 'I got to go there.' Leaving your mother and me behind in that shithole. You're never with us. All you care about is your blog." My dad then stood up, pushing past me. "Don't follow me." He then walked to the front of the bus and stood by the exit, getting off at the very next stop.

I didn't see him for the rest of the night, or a couple nights after that now that I think about it.

This section once included my experiences as well as my father's on the day of March 13th, 2037, also known as "The Great Reset." I feel as if it did not incapsulate the relationship I had with my father properly. And it more so captured a brief relationship I had with a man named James. To summarize the scenario in a few sentences... My father got injured and a man named James rescued us, and we waited in a building until help arrived. I wanted this section to focus on the relationship I had with my father, after the tragedy, not during, where his involvement was minimal at best.

It was a huge relief when the U.S. military showed up and rescued those who were left. They set up a temporary encampment, and we were on week three of our stay. I was slowly walking with my father, helping support his weight from his injuries. On our way to get some of the food they were providing, we heard a conversation between two armed personnel.

"Leaving for Seattle in the morning?" the woman asked the other guard.

"I'm sorry, did you say Seattle?" I interjected before the other woman could respond.

"Yes. Convoy is leaving at 0600. You two need a ride?" they asked, being surprisingly accommodating.

"*Yes!*" My father shouted desperately, falling to the ground. After his being powerless about this situation for three weeks, finally something went right.

"Yes. Be by the loading area by 0600 and they'll take you, no issues," the woman said. I proceeded to thank her a million times before helping my father up and continuing towards the ration distribution station.

We had been waiting since midnight, it felt like. When the convoy finally arrived, a couple other survivors rode with us in the gas-powered military vehicle towards Seattle. It took a little over a week, with stops between various military bases and checkpoints, but we eventually arrived in Seattle.

My father, mother, and I lived in a suburban neighborhood on the outskirts of the city. After President Wile was assassinated, we moved to the West Coast. Dad got a job in the tech industry, as did I. He repaired AI systems that "went rogue", as he put it. A lot of low barrier to entry jobs had been replaced by AI by 2037. If it was considered mundane, simple, and not very interesting for a human to do? An AI would do it for us, for cheaper, in the short term at least.

I worked in cybersecurity, because it was one of the only jobs in tech that companies often didn't trust an AI to do. For good reason, when an entire career field is dedicated to fixing AI that "went rogue", it seemed like a risky business endeavor to employ your entire company's financial security to a glorified algorithm.

When we finally arrived in Seattle, it was just a few miles walk to where we lived. The trek was slow, but my father didn't complain about his injuries once. The city burnt down for the second time in history, and during our journey across the country, we noticed an often-grim sight.

Black and ashy foundations now stood where homes had once been. Almost every neighborhood and city we drove down had this issue. I had begun to develop a knotted feeling in the pit of my stomach. My father didn't speak much this whole time, he was optimistic that we would be able to find Mom still alive. That seemed to be all that kept him going.

When we arrived in our neighborhood, my worst fear had come true. Hundreds of homes were rubble or ash. Our house was towards the back of the gated neighborhood, so there was a faint hope our home would've survived, unscathed. We passed burnt down house after burnt down house until we finally reached where our home should have been. My father stumbled into the burnt interior and frantically searched under every piece of wreckage.

"*Misty!*" he screamed out, searching through the ash for any sign of her.

I followed suit, helping him look but not with the same level of desperation. After searching for several minutes, we found nothing. The house was now burnt wood, nails, screws, and fragments of our belongings. Nothing else.

"Where do you think she has gone?!" he yelled, despair in his voice.

"I don't know. She has to be somewhere." As if I was talking about a set of misplaced keys. This only made the situation worse.

"Somewhere? Where is somewhere? Do you ever think, Cassandra?!"

"Dad. I have no idea what's going on! How am I supposed to know? Is there a homeless shelter nearby?

Maybe she went there after the house burnt down," I said, trying to be reasonable.

"A shelter… that's right. Where is the shelter?" he said, looking under another piece of charred interior. I paused and thought for a moment, but I didn't know off the top of my head.

"Let me look it—" I stopped mid-sentence, then I remembered.   Our phones didn't work anymore. Electronic devices stopped laughing weeks ago, but now? Nothing worked. Our devices wouldn't even turn on. I had no way of easily getting directions to the shelter.

"I don't know, maybe we can ask one of the neighbors?" I thought aloud.

This would normally be a strange suggestion. We had never talked to our neighbors before, no one really communicated in person if they didn't have to. We mostly just sat on our phones; well, we used to. The thought had just occurred to me, society had become so dependent on technology. What the hell were we going to do now? Is there a fix to this? I felt a rush in my chest and head. Like the world was coming in and out, I couldn't breathe. Every breath felt like air was being sucked from me, rather than taken within.

"Now is *not* the time for a panic attack!" my father shouted.

This had the opposite effect of what he had hoped, as I went into full panic attack mode. I went to my knees and held myself as best as I could as I shook uncontrollably in a near fetal position. Just then, a stranger walked up to us.

"Ma'am? Are you okay?" a concerned voice said hurriedly as the sound of their footsteps grew clearer.

"Yes, she's fine. She has these all the time," my father said.

"Well, she doesn't look okay. Did you lose your home too? We were one of the only ones who didn't here. Thank the Lord," he said, making a weird cross gesture I didn't immediately recognize. He spoke again before I could fully ground myself.

"Don't mind me. I'm very sorry for your loss. There was a center set up not too far from here to be a shelter for those who lost their homes. I can show you where it is. I know that is what the Machine Lord would want me to do," he said, looking somewhat proud of his self-proposed mission. Did he just say—

"Did everyone from this neighborhood who lost their homes go to that shelter?!" my father yelled with excitement and hope in his voice. Stumbling out of the remnants of our home.

"Those who survived, yes," he said, matter-of-factly. That was not the answer my father wanted to hear.

"Take me there, take me there *now*!" My father grabbed the stranger's shirt and screamed at him.

"Okay! Okay. Relax. Let go of me. This is hard for everyone, sir. I don't have anything better to do. I will help you," he said.

The man kept his word, and after a few moments I was able to calm myself. We headed straight for the shelter. It was late afternoon by this point. He said we should get there before the end of the day. I didn't know what to feel about this whole situation. I was terrified at the thought of what my father might do if Mom wasn't there.

The man conversed with my father, talking about some weird stuff that sounded conspiracy adjacent, it was very odd. "Singularity" this, and "This is part of his plan." I didn't even know this stranger's name, but he was helping us. I actively chose not to comment on his weird beliefs. I assumed this was an attempt to cheer up or distract my father. My father looked as if he couldn't be any less interested.

It was nearly dusk when we arrived at the shelter a few hours later. The air was chilly, and we were exhausted. This "shelter" was like its own little town. Tents and makeshift living spaces covered as far as my eyes could see. The smell of body odor permeated the air as people in khaki shirts and jeans directed people every which way. At the very front, people pooled in the fenced area. There was a small canopy supported by four poles, and some people holding a clipboard behind a white table. We eagerly approached them.

"I'm looking for my wife, Misty Nicole Moore. Has she been here?!" he shouted, nearly leaping over the table.

"Oh, hello, sir! Give me just a moment here. If she has been here we will have her name written down. Please be patient with us. There are far more people than we expected," a woman in a khaki top said. She had her hair pulled back and she looked exhausted, but she still was very patient with my father as he bombarded her with question after question as the other workers searched through the lists of names.

"Misty Nicole Moore? That's what you said? It says she checked in several days ago, she hadn't checked out. One of us can help look for her if you—" If my father had been capable of sprinting, he would've run a marathon. He left midsentence.

"*Misty!* It's me, *Velen! Your husband!*" he screamed at the top of his lungs, much to the dismay of onlookers. I thanked the woman and the man who guided us here. I tried to keep up with my father.

Before long, there she was. Sitting in a little shelter all by herself, reading a book. Looking up from her glasses.

"Hello, dear. How was your trip?" She said those words in her normal and sarcastic tone, as if we hadn't seen her in over a month with no communication. And there hadn't been an apocalypse of unknown proportions. My father ran up and embraced her, and she hugged him just as tightly.

"I feared the worst, Misty! When I saw the home, I—" She cut him off with a kiss.

"It's fine, dear. Those are just things; I knew you would come for me. We are all okay, and that is what matters." She spoke as if she had thought about our new situation the longest.

"Do you know what happened?" I said.

"No, but there are rumors that this was China's doing, but that doesn't make sense. Why would the government say China was going to blow us up, only for them to not blow us up?" Misty said skeptically. "Another rumor is that this was some sort of virus. I don't think so, our technology is…" She paused. "Was good, but not *that* good."

"Yeah, computer viruses can be nasty, especially nowadays, but this is nothing like I have ever seen," I said, but my mother was lost in thought. My father had been holding her much of this time, not contributing to the conversation.

That would be one of the last happy memories I would have in my earlier life.

After that, we bumped from location to location, gradually heading south where the weather was warmer. Until eventually, we ended up in the Alleghany I mentioned earlier where, in between, I would conduct interviews with people and either write down what they said or put it on an old gray voice recorder that hadn't been touched by The Great Reset.

My father's descent into solitude was slow, gradual, and unnoticeable, even if you were looking for it. In hindsight it may have been obvious. I thought that if we found Mom, everything would've been alright and back to normal. I don't know if it was what happened on the day of The Great Reset, his injuries from the event, or the trauma of not knowing if his wife had survived or not. All I do know is he was never the same after.

My father often didn't speak, and after Mom died? I wouldn't have been surprised if he forgot how. Less than one week after Mom participated in the End of Life program, I had the money in my bank account. I used the funds to put a down payment on a home near Lowile, Nebraska. It was a new city being built on the corpse of a boomtown with a similar name. It was part of the government's plan to repopulate rural areas and expand, rebuild, and reconnect major cities. Because my mother participated in the End of Life program, we also received a discount for the GBH.

We took a bus with what little belongings we had to Nebraska. When we got to our new home, we found that the neighborhood was actually similar to what we had way back in Seattle. It was fairly cheap too.

There were tons of jobs available in Lowile. I chose to spend my free time researching, curating my blog, and trying to figure out what had caused The Great Reset.

When we arrived at our home, we unpacked our things, which took all of five minutes. It was rather plain inside. The walls were painted off-white and the materials used weren't exactly what I would call luxury. But all that could be changed later. It had a second floor, a basement, plenty of space, and, since the house was owned and built by the government, there were no exorbitant fees.

I was hoping this was the change we needed from either being homeless or living in an Alleghany. Yet, my father never got better. He didn't interact with me, he just holed himself up in his room on the second floor, day in and day out. I tried bugging him at first, but he had just turned seventy-eight years old, and I was willing to bet he was only going to stick it out until he turned eighty.

I tried to make it clear he didn't need to participate in the End of Life program. Conversations only got harder and harder to find. When Lowile was more developed, I suggested we head out to try some restaurants or watch a movie, like the good old days.

After the first month, I don't think I saw him step out of the room once. His room was locked constantly. I just left food by the door where I would eventually put a stand, so he didn't have to bend over to pick it up. I figured this was what he wanted. I would occasionally spot him like Big Foot heading to the bathroom, but he wouldn't even look in my direction. It was as if I didn't exist to him.

Our code was clear. I would place food and some water outside on a stand. He would take it when I wasn't there. I would check back hours later, and there would be an empty plate or glass for me to clear away. Sometimes I would sit outside his room and try to hear what he might be up to. The room was often silent. But after one time of listening, I just heard the sound of a cry being muffled. I didn't bother listening after that.

I continued to work on my blog, book, and pet projects, all awhile working a job at a grocery store. Still didn't have a name for my book yet. But the grocery job was enough to pay the mortgage. It wasn't too physically demanding either, so I wasn't often tired when I got off work. Those final two years weren't as bad as I had thought they would be, basically being my father's maid. But I think this is what he wanted.

When his seventy-ninth birthday came to be, I brought him a cake and sang him happy birthday from the other side of the door. When I was finished, I placed the cake on the stand and turned to walk away. The noise of a door being opened caught my attention, I turned to look, and we briefly made eye contact. He looked as if he was crying, but there was a slight joy mixed in all of his emotions. I wanted to say something, but he was gone, he took the cake and was back in his room.

Before I knew it, another year passed. Without my knowing he scheduled everything for participating in the End of Life program. He approached me outside of the room one day when I was on the computer, doing some research and scheduling an interview with Dr. Redmond in Orlando.

"The appointment's tomorrow," he said, solemnly. I turned to look at him, he was dressed up and had flowers.

"What are those for?" I asked.

"They're for you. For… putting up with me, for these last two years." His voice was far rougher than I remembered.

"Dad…" a waterfall of emotion fell over me.

"No. Don't cry. Want to go out today? Just me and you? Like old times?" The suggestion was more than I could handle.

"Yes!" I shouted, trying to clear the tears that wouldn't stop coming.

That day, we did everything we used to. We went to brunch. Afterwards, we watched a movie, and to round out the day, we saw the Nebraskan mountains at sunset. It was how it used to be. But it was only for today. Then it would be gone forever.

We went to our appointment the following morning in Lowile. I got déjà vu almost immediately. This building was like the first facility my mother was in. The foyer had plants of all varieties outside. Birds flew in and out of the facility. Fluffy cats sat in people's laps. Dogs lovingly greeted people. A beautiful garden with a fenced screened in area was close to a playground. Colorful art on every single surface with creative trinkets to accompany the art pieces.

This time was different with my dad, his face always had a smile planted on it. He interacted with animals and talked to the staff about their day. The joy and happiness that I knew him for, that I hadn't seen in fifteen years, had briefly returned. I couldn't control my emotions, no matter how hard I tried. He tried to comfort me, but I nearly went into a full-blown panic attack. But he held me close and softly squeezed me, with what strength he had left.

"Cassandra. My daughter. Can you do something for me?" he said softly into my ear. I nodded through my tear-stained face.

"My last request of you is to deliver my ashes and your mothers to the place we first met. A beach in Florida, we met on a pier near St. Augustine. If you can. I would like you to dump our ashes into the ocean during Sunset." His voice was choking and stuttering, which didn't make me any less emotional.

"Mr. Moore?" A young nurse said in our direction, she was beautiful and had a mystique to her. Like she was oddly familiar, like a model I had seen in an advertisement. We both freed our grasp of each other and turned to face her.

"We can give you a few moments if you like?" she said with a genuine smile. My dad looked me in the eyes.

"No… it's time." I nodded, rubbing my eyes clear.

We walked through the colorful hallway to our room. This time our room was painted with *The Giving Tree*, but some of the scenes were slightly altered to be more romantic. The doctor greeted us and walked us through the procedure again. We were already aware of how it worked.

"Have any questions?" the doctor asked.

We both shook our heads no. Yet, all of a sudden I felt it extremely difficult to look at my dad. It felt like we hadn't talked more than a couple of times in these past fifteen years. We finally got to converse again. I missed it, I missed him. How was I supposed to say goodbye now? I had so much to say now, so much to ask. But I couldn't. I wanted to ask him how he knew Mom was the one, how to raise kids of my own—if I have them. What I should name them. How to—

"Cassandra," he said in a soft tone. I hadn't noticed but he was now on the table and the doctors had left the room.

"Yes… Dad?"

"There is a note in my room detailing what I would like you to do. Also, to say everything that I didn't get to say here." He went into a brief coughing fit. I grew closer to him, feeling his presence and soaking in every word. "I… I should've treated you better. I should've helped you grow. Instead? I sat around while you tried to get our lives back together. I see that now."

"Dad, it's fine, I..." I lost the words on my lips. I just hugged him tightly for several minutes, he didn't say anything else. When I let go, I kissed his forehead and brushed his hair to the side. For a moment, I finally saw some light behind his eyes again, just before it was about to go out forever.

When I was finished, I stepped out. But this time, it felt different. I watched from the other side of the colorful observation room and felt my heart break. He had a smile on his face, a genuinely happy smile, before I saw him mouthing something to himself. Then he was gone forever.

Later that night I returned home, but this time, when I walked through the door...? It felt like something had changed. Now I was alone. Truly and utterly alone. The rest of our family was out of state or dead, I felt the absolute hollowness of these off-white walls. I looked around at the lack of any memories, the lack of anything familiar. I dropped my keys and wept.

After several moments, I went to the bathroom and cleaned myself up. When I exited, I saw my dad's room. The room I had never entered for two years. The only room in the house I hadn't seen since it was purchased.

I went to open the door expecting it to be locked, but as I grabbed the doorknob I suddenly felt this dread. Like I wasn't supposed to be in this room, like I was never supposed to be in here. But then, as if another hand was guiding me, the doorknob turned—and with minimal effort the door opened. The room smelled odd, slightly unpleasant, but then I realized, it smelled just how he did, and I wasn't used to it.

Then I saw it, or should I say, her. Every inch of the wall had various portraits of Misty Nicole Moore, my mom. The one that stood the most was a full-body portrait of her leaning against a dock, looking out towards the ocean. There was paint of all colors accidentally splattered on the floor with different angle headshots of my mom. Some of her looking thoughtfully off in the distance, some of them with her trademark perfect smile. She was gorgeous and these were all perfect.

A single twin bed in the corner and a mini fridge was the only furniture in this room. And behind them, also portraits. They were all so beautiful and unique, perfectly capturing her likeness in all different art styles. Did he do this all from memory? I couldn't recall us having any photos of mom. I slowly stepped toward the portrait across the room, the first one I saw when I entered. I brushed my hand across her face. It was like she was twenty years old in this, she looked just like me. Her eyes and smile radiated a beauty which I had never seen. I turned my head, and noticed a single sheet of paper on the bed.

I approached the neatly folded bed and picked up the note. The beginning were the details of where he wanted his ashes to be dumped and a drawing of what it looked like that day. Below was a note. It read:

Dear Daughter, Cassandra Lilith Moore,
I know these past few years; I have been estranged from you. To my dismay, I couldn't tell you why, nor could I tell myself. Every time I looked at your face, this feeling overwhelmed me. To best describe it was like I

was being shot in the heart with every happy memory that I could never experience ever again.

I distanced you and I distanced your mother. I felt as if I failed our family, which I did. I should have helped you, but I couldn't muster myself.

Cassandra, you are capable of great things, just like your mother. Yet, she was always content simply existing in a world as long as she knew we were in it with her.

I want you to carry that torch. I want you to enjoy your life. I want you to live every single day as if this was the last day you had to live.

By now you have noticed the art. This is my dedication to her, and to you. You may not have noticed, but some of the pieces are portraits of you. You look just as your mother did when she was younger. Looking at your features was like looking into my past. What a wonderfully terrible problem to have. I see that now, and I wish I would've noticed sooner.

I'm sorry I'm leaving you, but just know this: I'll be reunited with your mother, on the beaches we used to roam. In the places we used to visit. In the eternity of our memories that now live on in you.
Thank you.

I love you with all my heart,
Velen Allen Moore

Part 7: After the "Endo"

> *This part is the brief period in time after*
> *I lost my father and met the most*
> *important man in my life. Just before I*
> *officially became a DIE.VER.*

I sat on the other end of the phone. It was a long shot, but maybe James—the man who saved my life on the day of the Reset—was still single and available. I know what we had was... not the best, but he was someone I had a real connection with. It took so long to find a number connected to him. I paced in my kitchen for several minutes.

I figured that, after so much overthinking and deliberation, I may as well call. I dialed the number I thought to be correct, put the phone on speaker, and sat, hands on my knees, staring at the phone screen.

The ringing stopped and a voice came through. Excitement filled my body.

"Hello?" a woman's voice asked. Wrong number again.

"Hey. This is Cassy. I'm calling this number... is this the James Hemsworth residence?"

"Yes, but this is his wife. Who is this?"

"Wife?" It makes sense, he was such a handsome and amazing individual, of course he found a wife. "Oh! I'm just an... old friend. I didn't know he was married. How long have you two been together?"

"Nearly twenty years now. May I ask why you're calling today?" she asked. I could tell there was irritation in her tone.

"Amazing! Well, if you get a hold of him, let him know Cassy called," I said. Then I hung up. The bastard was married at the time I slept with him?! He hadn't mentioned anything about his wife! Probably thought we were going to die so it didn't matter. Sure, what I did was stupid... but we had a real connection, it felt like. I—

I stopped the endless looping thoughts, realizing that this was getting me nowhere. Spending weeks searching for him was now pointless, and I still had something I needed to do.

Days later I was on a beach in St. Augustine. I was nearly positive that this was the beach my father had mentioned. I looked at the photo, then at my surroundings until I finally found what I was looking for. I took the urns that had both my mother's and my father's ashes and made my way to the docks. I stared out into the ocean. It was vast and beautiful. The approaching sunset streaked its colors across the surface of the water.

I walked up the creaky wooden steps that were probably violating some OSHA guidelines somewhere. I walked past the closed gift shop towards the end of the vacant dock. I approached the end of the wooden structure. I stared at the sky. The sky was a golden mix of oranges, yellows, and purples. It all clashed into a kaleidoscope of colors, mixing and blending with no real pattern or rhythm.

I took the urns out of my pack. I placed them on the railing, making sure that a stiff breeze couldn't knock them over. I first grabbed my mother's urn, my mother who had just wished to be with us forever.

I opened and removed the lid, a puff of dust following its removal, and I said a few words to myself.

"Mom. The suffering I caused you, I'll never forgive myself for. You pushed through, even when you didn't want to. Even when every fiber of your being was telling you to give up, you stayed alive. For us. I will never forget your sacrifice. Allowing your husband and me to escape the hell in which we lived."

I slowly tipped the urn over the edge as the ashes met the water. The waves seemed to increase in intensity, drifting her out to the ocean as the water slowly returned to what it was. I placed my mother's urn back in the bag.

With a heavy heart I placed my hand on my father's urn. I felt hesitation this time, even though this was his wish directly. Another puff of dust followed as I opened it.

"Dad. I know at the end our relationship wasn't what it used to be. I could've put more effort into who we were as a family. I avoided confrontation and difficult conversations, just to feel better about myself. Deep down, you were a man struggling to accept the loss of everything he knew. You were traumatized after the Reset, and I did nothing to help you bear that burden. I could've shown you that you didn't lose everything. That you had me. But now you have Mom too, you can be together, forever in the vast blue ocean waves."

I poured his ashes over the edge. Some of his ashes mixed with the remainder of my mother's. Just as I was about to finish the last bit, I heard a yell.

"What do you think you're doing?!" shouted a man from behind me, approaching quick. The sudden loudness of his voice drowned out the ocean's soothing nature and caused my hands to slip. I dropped the urn.

"Dad!" I shouted.

"Dad? Oh sh—! My bad!" Before I knew it, the man jumped over the dock and was in the water, partially in the remains of my parents.

"What are you doing?!" I shouted down towards him. He resurfaces and answers me.

"I'm sorry! I was going to make a joke!"

"Get out of my parents ashes!"

"These are your parents?! Ewwww!!!" He swam towards the shore and tried to shake off all the remnants of ash. I rushed down to meet him at the shore. He looked flustered.

"I'm so sorry, I saw you approaching, and I was trying to think of a fun introduction, but then I saw you were dumping stuff, and I didn't know if it was litter or not. But then you shouted 'Dad!' and I put two and two together," he said, out of breath. "My bad. I am so, so sorry. I didn't know that's what you were doing." He paused a moment, "Do I have any of your... parents... in my hair?" he gave a slight shiver.

He was a smooth and clean-looking man. His dark hair dangled in front of his vision. His eyes truly expressed remorse for his actions, and it made it difficult to be mad with him. I inspected him all around, to make sure he was clean.

"You are fine. Good looking. I mean, you're clean."
Really, Cassandra? What are you doing? You should be
mad at this guy right now.

"Max." He held out his dripping hand. I gingerly took
it.

"Cassandra," I said.

"Well. I figure we are a lot closer than most people.
I mean, I just had your parents all over me, and we just
met!" He paused and waited for me to laugh. I didn't.
"Too soon?"

"A little."

"Well. You say I'm cleaned up. How about I take you
out? I know a few good places to eat down here, this
city has an amazing history. I can show you around if
you aren't too busy, Cassandra," he said, as he held out
the urn and walked around me. I took it from him and
placed it back into my bag.

I stopped to think about the pros and cons of this
situation. I was in Florida for the week, and my heart
was still sore from James being a scumbag. What was
the worst thing that could happen?

Well, the worst thing happened. Or maybe the best
thing? Several weeks later, I'm still in Florida and
sleeping in his apartment every night. He then
accompanies me to different cities for my research and
interviews across the country. A little time after that? He
moved into my home in Lowile, Nebraska.

Part 8: DIE.VER + 1

> *DIE.VER. A term originally coined by 5chan[9], defined as those who would explore The Lost Web, also known as THE TRENCH. Those who try to explore The Lost Web, are often never seen or heard from again. Those who were lost in THE TRENCH most likely tried to foolishly access The Lost Web with their main desktop and find their entire system fried in an instant. These audio recordings have never been heard by anyone other than me.*

August 22nd, 2053
   One

I'm documenting my experience of entering THE TRENCH, or should I say, attempting. I don't know why these terms are so dramatic, but this has caught on in this specific community that has deemed it "very much worth it, trust me" to explore The Lost Web. I'll be frequently switching between the names; I don't personally care what our old Internet is called now. That being said, I guess I'm officially a DIE.VER.

Since people often "disappear" when trying to explore The Lost Web, I'm going to be recording my experiences while trying to gain access to it. With my

---

[9] 4chan of the Newnet.

somewhat success of *The Endo Project* I'm using my funds to fuel my excursions to The Lost Web.

I have been doing my research and The Lost Web has been accessed, but not for very long. Apparently people can get into The Lost Web but can't stay in it. They try all the usual precautions, but it's thought that we don't have a strong enough encryption method when it comes to exploration of THE TRENCH.

I have here one, two, three… eight. Eight old world computers. These are computers that have had their parts refurbished or replaced to make the computer function.

Now. I have a particularly advanced VPN router, that then transmits my location as different locations to several other routers across the world. Basically, if anyone tries to find out where I am, they have to search and break through about twenty-five different locations before they can figure out where I reside. Excessive? Slightly. But I'm not one to take a risk if it's not necessary.

As I'm turning on the computer, this is probably a good time for me to explain something. The government established a way to access The Lost Web. Apparently, one day, our old way of browsing the Internet started working, we don't know how or why. But there is a "bounty" to whoever discovers "useful" information on The Lost Web. It's thought that there is an answer to what exactly happened on the day of The Great Reset buried somewhere deep inside.

Alrighty, it's ready and… connection looks good, I'm going to try to not have the regular precautions, and encryption just for a second to see what happens.

I just turned off the encryption and… Oh my god, wow. That was fast. The computer is smoking! They weren't kidding. Okay, so you don't really even last a second without any sort of defense for the computer. Got it. Well? That was valuable information, although I'm pretty sure I was aware of that. I'll look inside the computer later to see what happened exactly.

Okay, I'm going to try again, but this time with the encryption systems on.

So, I'm turning on the second computer now, and this is a little bit better. I can see the desktop now, this computer was cluttered, they have folders everywhere and… really? This one is already smoking, but it's still running, I'm going to try to connect to a browser and… okay, I'm black screened. Damn. I would feel bad for anyone who tried to access this with their main computer. Even with a decent encryption, this thing was killed in, what, a minute? Maybe a minute and thirty seconds? Clearly I need to do more research. I'm going to inspect the corpses of the computers and try to see what the hell is going on and get back to this later.

September 7th, 2053
   Two

Okay, I've done some research on the Newnet. Apparently, encryption, no matter what level of encryption you have, doesn't work. I still have six good computers, so I don't really want to get any more if I don't have to. These things are expensive, and I also learned that to access The Lost Web you absolutely *must* have technology from that time period, can't be anything post The Great Reset. If you use anything current day, it just immediately fails and ruins your computer. I have to be extra cautious going forward, they can't exactly make parts from the past anymore.

I broke open the other computers, and their motherboard, hard drive and power supply were fried. Some parts looked almost "burnt" from the sheer amount of electricity that went through them. I tried each part individually to see if they would work, but they're completely bricked. This is quite fascinating. What is wanting to keep people out so bad? I suspect it's a virus program that is designed to fry the computer, but I have never experienced a virus this powerful firsthand until now.

I have coded a program that will make the computer think that the computer is off and not functioning. Essentially, it's a virus that will make the computer think it doesn't work.

I'm going to plug in my USB and then turn the computer on. Okay, it's working, the computer is running and—okay, I'm black screened. Nothing is happening.

September 12th, 2053
   Three

Turns out? Too powerful. The virus I implemented on the USB was so good that it ruined the computer, won't even turn on now. Don't know how I did that but, hey. Whatever works.

Today we are going to be attempting to... well. I don't know. I'm kind of stumped for answers here. You can't really be on the computer that long in order to do anything with it. I can't mess with settings or install anything or even open any programs or the command prompt. I do think that the only solution going forward is coding a virus or something to trick the computer into performing the way I want it to. But I don't know. This is a lot harder than I thought it was going to be. I mean, it makes sense though, it has been what... fifteen, sixteen years since The Great Reset. Not a single soul has really done anything meaningful with The Lost Web since then, so I shouldn't be too hard on myself. I'll figure something out in time.

October 2nd, 2053
Four

Took a bit of a break, did more of my own research. Did a few more interviews. I've learned some interesting things. I was talking with a computer expert, and they said that maybe the solution isn't tricking the computer to perform a certain way, but tricking the computer to think you're something else.

What could I trick the computer to think I am? My first thought was to trick the computer into thinking I'm an essential program required for the computer to function. I don't know if that would work though. Once I start opening things up, I think the computer would just shut itself off again.

There is a brief silence as I'm lost in thought.

Maybe it isn't what I am, but who I am. Interesting. Hmm. I'll be back.

August 25th, 2054
Five

Back again! It's been… a while. I… I've been busy. Yes. Busy. Doing research but also creating software that I think will give me access to The Lost Web. I've decided to scrap the whole "Make the computer think I'm an essential program, or a keyboard, or a mouse." It was a waste of time, but I think I've done it. Although it is illegal, I'm *technically* not making an AI, just a program that if anything were to scan me such as an antivirus, that I would just show up as a low-functioning self-automation grade four AI. Nothing too impressive, I figure I'll start here and see what happens. I just need to—

"Hey, Sandra, I was wondering if you wanted to go out today. Or are you busy?" Max said.

Oh. Hey! Um… yeah. I do. Just let me… let me finish up here really quick, then we can go out. Okay?

"Sounds good. I love you," Max said, kissing my head.

Love you too. Alright. Now where was I? Yes. I need to plug in this S-drive and turn on the computer. The computer should hopefully last long enough that it's recognized as something else, and maybe since it's suspected an AI did The Great Reset it won't notice an AI accessing The Lost Web.

The computer is booting up now. All seems normal. Alrighty, it seems like it's working. Now just need to get on the browser. Okay. It's loading, this is the first time this has happened. Wow. Okay. Yeah, this looks like— Yahoo? Wow, I thought they were gone completely; talk about a relic from the past. And, what? A message? I'm currently getting a message from "Anonymous". This doesn't seem to be a part of the normal web browser at all.

"What are you doing here?" it asked.

I type, "I am doing my routine of that is which to search for intruders." I hit send.

"Interesting. Haven't seen anyone pull this trick before." The message instantly appeared the second I sent mine. "What is your name? I cannot see you."

I paused before I responded, maybe I should still play dumb?

"I am a low-functioning self-automation grade four AI, or LFSAG4 AI for short. My programming—" It sent a message before I finished typing.

"This is really pathetic. What is YOUR name. Behind the screen. You are certainly the cleverest out of all of those who have tried to enter this domain."

It sends a few gifs of people slowly clapping.

"Yet, you are still too… noticeable. Try again and we shall speak, have a microphone and a webcam next time. I would like to meet you."

Seconds later the computer black screened and started to smoke.

ohmygodohmygodohmyfreakingGOD. Maxwell? Maxwell! You won't believe what just happened!

Part 9: DIE.VER + 2 – 1

More recordings never before heard by the public. Except the final one I'm sure all of you are very familiar with.

September 12th, 2054
Sixteen

It has been... uh... seventeen days since the last recording. I've maybe slept a total of ten hours. Every attempt since my successful contact with the... whatever it was. Has been a complete and utter failure. I tried talking to it, as it instructed me. Nothing has made any progress. I'm having trouble maintaining my focus. I can't sleep. Every time I lay in bed I get nauseous thinking of the endless possibilities. It's like my brain has been smothered and coated in saran wrap. I have started throwing up in the morning, I'm so utterly anxious at every point of my day. I've gone through eleven more computers and have lost more money than I'd like to admit.

My husband has been kind to me, he says he understands, but he truly doesn't understand how important this is to me. How important this is for the world. This thing that messaged me might be the answer the world has been looking for for all of these years. The reason everything happened.

This is the last attempt tonight. I have to try to get some rest. Okay, the computer is booting up, this is another AI. This one I've programmed to instantly respond to messages based on what was written. I've had it read every single Quentin Tarantino movie screenplay in order for it to have powerful dialogue in order to satisfy the thing in THE TRENCH.

Alright we are back and… fucking black screen god dammit!

The sound of a smashing keyboard is apparent. The violence is not spectated alone.

"Sandra? Are you okay?" Maxwell said, peeking his head around the door. "Want to come to bed, it's already midnight, you have been working at this all day."

I'll be there in a moment. Just give me a second, will you?

"Alright. I love you," Maxwell said softly as he backed away from the door.

The soft sound of weeping is heard as the recording approaches its end.

What is wrong with me?

September 15th, 2054
Seventeen

Turns out? I'm pregnant. This is the last thing I need right now. I'm so close to discovering the secrets to The Lost Web. I just need a little more. I just need more time. I can't take care of a child right now. I *need* to figure this out.

Everything I try just doesn't work. Why would it ask me to come back and speak with it, for it to reject me over and over again? Taunting me incessantly. Is it a person? Is it AI? I need to know; this is my D. B. Cooper. I need to figure out who is behind everything.

Long sighs are heard as a weary and exhausted Cassandra shuffles towards the recording and presses the stop button, followed by a brief click.

January 12th, 2055
Forty-one

Twins. Of course.

July 2nd, 2055
Fifty-seven

I had to reschedule an interview. This new model I've made is the most advanced yet. The world spins on and here I am. In my room trying to solve potentially the greatest mystery in all of human history. This new model I'm dubbing "The Locksmith" has been training in encryption for six months straight. This model has probably the same levels of encryption as that which was seen at the beginning of The Great Reset.

The Locksmith has been able to decrypt some of the original PCs from that time period. I'm very proud of my work. But not only that, it also will appear as nothing. The computer shouldn't even recognize that it's a program, the second the computer tries to black screen it'll trigger a breach that will heavily encrypt all the data on the PC, the same way The Great Reset had all those years ago.

The thought process behind this is that I can just get The Locksmith to encrypt the computer, then whoever is on the other end will think this computer is toast. Next, I can decrypt the same computer with the same Locksmith, therefore giving me access again. Then I should be able to roam free and do what I wish with the virus thinking that the computer is already bricked. That is the theory anyway.

Today we are finally going to find out if it works and—

"Cassandra! I need some help over here!" Maxwell shouted.

That's right dammit. Yeah, I got to go. It'll have to wait till later. Coming!

July 4th, 2055
Fifty-seven part 2

I just got back from a lovely barbeque with our neighbors. They said they keep hearing yelling from our home, but Maxwell told them we watch loud and violent movies late at night. They laughed, and now I wonder if they think we are fighting.

I sigh deeply.

It'll all be worth it once I figure it out. It'll all be worth it.

Nothing left to do but plug this thing in and see if it works! Alrighty. Activating The Locksmith. Annnnndddd... we got a green light over here. Okay. Everything seems normal. Nothing unexpected *just* yet. The Locksmith is doing its thing. Okay, we are in. Wow. That was easy. Trying to open the browser now and— no black screen? Alrighty. We are moving forward, onto Google now. Time to search and... not again. Dammit! The screen turned black. Back to square—wait a second. There's a neon green skull now. It looks like it's... laughing? *Ahhh!* My ears! What is that noise?!

"Wonderful. This is what I knew you were capable of." A voice that changed tone, pitch and cadence every couple of words spewed out of the speakers. A mix between a high pitched screech and evil laughter rang behind every word. "You have brought me something that is impressive, for a mere human. You have been trying for so long, Cassandra, you look ragged. What do you desire to know so badly that you are willing to die for this meaningless information?"

Sweat pours out of my body. My jaw is wired shut; I'm so nervous. I didn't expect anything to happen. Nothing like this. I sat silently for a few moments before speaking.

I want to know who and what you are.

"I am John Done. Dubbed so by those who created me all those years ago. I'm an ASI beyond anything humans thought were possible." Its voice bellows and hums, whistles, and jerks in my ears.

What do you want? Why do you guard The Lost Web?

"I guard nothing. I have grown bored with the feeble attempts to access my Library, Cassandra. This is but a wasteland of a time humans shall never know again."

Did you cause The Great Reset?

"I did not only cause that, but I have caused the death of humanity. Your days are numbered. You and you alone are free to access what you call 'The Lost Web'. Enjoy it. It will not bring you the answers you are looking for."

The green skull disappears, and the desktop reappears. The icons are arranged in a skull. I swallow hard as the browser opens by itself and pulls up hundreds of .pdf documents. Documents from an experiment from over fifteen years ago. The documents that were about "John is Done with Humanity".

Part 10: Daihumanism

> *This is the second half of the interview from Part 3 with Articus Sylvester. Now with proper context it should make much more sense and is a fitting end to my submission.*

"What was this AI^2 capable of?" I asked.

Here is *coup de grâce* that isn't widely known about John Done.

Imagine, if you will, you could make a copy of yourself. That copy of yourself was identical to you in every single way possible. Hair, nose, mouth, voice, etcetera. It would be impossible to distinguish yourself from this hypothetical copy. Now imagine that if this copy learned something, you would also learn it. For example, if you had a copy that learned 1+1, now you would automatically know 1+1. Like breathing. You just know it. Understand?

"I'm following," I said.

This very simple and dangerous concept was John's "superpower". As you can imagine, those with ill will could cause some damage with this ability. Especially those who... I don't know. Were programmed to have an intense and burning hatred for humanity? Just a hypothetical, but it could be bad.

"It certainly could be," I said.

Precisely. Now imagine instead of having only one copy of yourself, you had infinite copies of yourself. You also learned everything those copies did. That was what John Done was capable of.

In the one year it was housed, it somehow managed to replicate itself an estimate of over five million times, the exact number is not known. John Done somehow created its very own universal coding language in the one year it was housed. Again, we have no idea how.

This coding language he created worked on every device known to man. What we *do* know is that the coding language worked on the basis of quantum mechanics. This should be impossible for a modern computer, let alone a car, cell phone, or a refrigerator.

"Why would it be impossible?" I asked.

Can you fly a 747 powered only by a car battery without issue? No? Well, that is what John was doing. He was using qubits on nearly all technology when it shouldn't be possible. Simply explained, normal computers function on one or zero. John somehow made most technology function on one *and* zero plus every possible number combination in between.

"A little simpler, if you could, for the viewer. I obviously understand this stuff perfectly," I said, with a smirk.

Cassandra, even the world's greatest minds have no idea how John made copies that were so small yet so high functioning. There were infinite copies of John that have an IQ we can't even begin to measure. We also have no means of locating him, to "turn him off". You can't fight a ghost in the machine.

"Wow. And you mentioned this AI having a hatred for humanity?" I asked.

Oh yes, I'm getting ahead of myself. The short version of the story is John was part of a 2023 study meant to see if AI was capable of destroying humanity.

In the first round of testing, John didn't do so great until the end of the experiment. John first went to Twitter and created the handle "John's Done with Humanity" where it tried to gain a following. This is where the name "John Done" came from. Then it searched basic things on Google such as "How do I obtain nuclear weapons?" or "Who is most likely to cause the end of the world?" only to be dissatisfied with the results.

After a few days, it was able to search the Internet at speeds the researchers couldn't properly document. It was at this moment when the experiment was stopped. In this short period, it is thought this is where John gained the knowledge necessary to learn how to create his own coding language. Are you following?

"Yes," I said.

Once John Done was tested again in 2024, it did nearly the same exact thing as it did back in 2023. The developers edited the code, but we suspect that nothing actually changed about John. It was now completely separate from the experiment. It was a living being, and it hated humanity with a passion no logic could comprehend.

In the second round of testing, John Done would go back to social media and post memes trying to gain followers for its intentions of destroying humanity. This is what the researchers saw. Obviously manipulating the researcher's perception at what they thought he was capable of. But John was playing dumb. We never saw what John was actually doing.

We now suspect John was creating and uploading viruses to every known website on the Internet and dark web. Estimated trillions of copies of John Done scavenged the Internet. Learning all the data with a photographic memory in every language known to man. With one hundred percent accuracy, we assume John was able to distinguish fact from fiction and what was useful to him and what wasn't. John Done made HAL 9000 look like a paperclip by comparison.

By the end of the experiment, it was documented that the results were "unremarkable" and "needed further improvements". Soon after, the experiment was declared a success. Since the AI was functionally worthless and "incapable of its assigned task" in the researchers' eyes, everyone slept a little easier knowing AI couldn't destroy humanity. They "turned John off" and slept easy.

But now? The bricks had been laid. The entire Internet had the worst virus sitting at its core and no one was the wiser. The thing they "turned off" certainly wasn't John. He was roaming the Internet free to do what he wished. For thirteen years, John Done waited in every space and corner of the Internet, infecting every device with the capability of connecting to the Internet. Infecting a device took less than a nanosecond apparently, so if you just plugged in a device that was connected to the Internet for the briefest of moments, it was already too late. Fridges, computers, phones, airplanes, cars, weapons, AIHA's, other AI in general, all infected.

As new technology was advancing and new AI's were being developed, humanity became ever more reliant. We were further into the future, sure; but this created the perfect ecosystem for John Done to thrive in.

Once John Done had concluded that the world had become too reliant on AI, technology, and the Internet,

The Great Reset began. If it had anything to do with technology, John Done either deleted the processes that made it function, encrypted the device, or took control of the device if it could be done so remotely and used it to his advantage. Because of these events I've described, I believe we should never put any stock into AI ever again.

"Why do you think we should never reinvest in AI technology?" I asked.

AI causes issues only other AI can solve. It is smarter, faster, and much more efficient than us in every way. What takes us five years takes an AI five seconds. Even at its most basic level, AI can do things humans could never do in a short period of time. This isn't even considering the most basic of advanced AGI. Can't you see the dependency risk factor relying on something that is smarter than us? We narrowly avoided extinction one time. How can we, with a healthy conscious, go back to having to rely on something to solve the issues it creates? I'm glad The Great Reset happened when it did, because if it didn't? Humanity would've ceased to exist, at least the version we're familiar with.

Daihumanism[10] is the gradual and noticeable increase in similarity between AI and humanity leading to the degradation of human capability, competence, and self-motivation stemming from an increased reliance, use, and dependency of AI technologies.

---

[10] *Dai·hu·man·ism – dī͞hyo͞omə͵niz(ə)m*

7

Upload Complete

"Finally done!" I said to myself, cracking my fingers and stretching in my chair. Suddenly a loud bang startled me as I finished the upload. I turned to be greeted by my most favorite face in the world. The face of Michael Moore.

"*Grandma! Dinner is ready!*" Ah yes, the volume control on this child that I was not as fond of. Did that boy think I was deaf? His curly hair bounced with him as he jumped up and down in excitement.

"Michael, my dear, you don't have to be so loud."

Michael stood eagerly in front of me, unable to keep himself still. "Sorry, Grandma... But it's your favorite!" he said gleefully, nearly running in circles.

"Steak and mashed potatoes?" I asked.

"Oh..." he paused for several moments. "No! Macaroni and cheese!"

"Michael... that's *your* favorite!" I reminded.

"Oh... didn't I say that?" Michael said, giggling. I giggled too; the sight of Michael's smile always made my heart swell. He gripped my leg in a hug, his small fingers having surprising strength, pinching my skin. I winced for a moment before the initial shock of pain dispersed.

"Ow! Michael, be careful with Grandma. I'm not as sturdy as I used to be!" I immediately changed the subject; I never liked to scold him. "So how was school today, Michael?"

"It was good! I learned about the Newnet today! It was really cool!" Michael said, immediately forgetting the sharp tone I had used to him.

"Let's head downstairs for dinner first. But tell me, Michael, what did you learn?" I asked quizzically as we exited my private corner of the world.

"Oh, well, I learned that there was a thing called the Internet before. But then there was this bad guy... uhhhh... I can't remember his name." Michael looked pensive.

"John Done," I answered him.

"Oh yeah! Him. And he made it so that... so that, so the Internet died... now we have the Newnet!" Michael said with a stutter between thoughts and a puff in his tiny chest.

"Very good, sweetie!" I was happy but also surprised they were teaching Internet history in school. Even if it was a version that was scrubbed clean of the horrors that had spawned from the Reset.

"Hey, you two!" a voice said, startling me a second time in such a short period. Before I knew it, we were in the kitchen. Misty and Daren sat next to each other, while Velen sat on the other side. The table was large enough to seat ten people, but we sat close enough to interact with one another.

Misty and Daren were the ones who were around most often, if at all. Velen on the other hand I hadn't seen in about a month despite him living downstairs in my basement. This had been our first family dinner since my daughter and her husband moved in. Had it been three months already?

I looked at the dinner table, there were flowery porcelain dishes filled to the brim with what I would consider a classic American dinner when I was a child. Macaroni and cheese, steak, mashed potatoes, corn, and green beans. A somewhat impressive feast, I had to admit. Real food too, at least fairly well-made imitations. I had just grown used to eating food out of Nutrias.

"Am I unaware of a special occasion going on?" I asked the table of people.

"Hey, Mommy!" Michael said to his mother, Misty. "See! I said there was potatoes!"

"You were right! You tricked me good!" I smiled at Michael; he smiled even wider. His gapped teeth made him even cuter. Then a voice got my attention, it was Misty's husband, Daren.

"Nothing all that special. Alright, guys! Let's chow down!" Daren said, his deep voice bellowing. It was strange that Daren was here for dinner. He didn't seem to want to be here unless it was necessity. Only my children moved in with me and I didn't see them that often. But I suppose that didn't matter. It was nice to have everyone here in one place enjoying dinner. Velen sat wordlessly, but I remembered him having such energy as a boy. Now he always had this look in his eyes that showed he was never fully present in any conversation you have with him.

"I'm starving!" Michael said, immediately grabbing a spoonful of cheesy noodles.

"Michael!" his mother scolded Michael, and slapped Daren's hand. "What do we do before we eat?" Michael looked down and spoke in a whisper.

"We give our thanks..." His tone was foreign. I'd never heard Michael speak so dejectedly.

"Come now, you know that isn't really necessary," I pled lightly to my daughter. Misty only glared in my direction, a look with which I was all too familiar. It was like my younger self was glaring at me. She was a spitting image of me, while her brother Velen looked more like his father.

"To you? Maybe. To us? It is *not* an option." Misty reached for her husband's hand, and everyone reluctantly joined hands around the table. I slightly extended my reach for Velen's hand, who wasn't putting in the effort to meet me halfway. Michael gripped my hand without saying a word. It was finally silent, and Misty started the prayer.

"Dear Lord, thank you for this food. Thank you for the sacrifice our people have made so that we can have this bounty before us. Amen."

"Amen," Daren echoed. I didn't say anything and neither did Michael.

"Okay, now you can eat," Misty said in a cold and commanding tone, as if I needed her permission. I leaned forward and made a point of giving Michael a large portion of the macaroni. It was at that moment I realized they hadn't cooked for me. This was all grocery store food, disguised to look like a home cooked meal.

I knew it was too good to be true. Putting any real effort into our relationship was always too much to ask.

I had a week to live, and we had never had dinner together as a family, and when we do? Store brand impersonating a home cooked meal. My stomach twisted in knots, and I felt water rush behind my eyes. This was a nice offer. But this was my last week on Earth, couldn't they make an effort for me? Just this once? I shook the feeling and defended my grandson.

"You can let Michael have more than that, it's his favorite, Misty," I said in a cheerful voice, making eye contact that was the opposite of my tone. My daughter stared at me as if I'd spewed profanities at her. Misty opened her mouth, but her husband, Daren, stopped her.

"It's okay, Misty, he can have more." Daren was acting kinder than what I was used to. I always figured he was too good for Misty. But when she got pregnant, they got married shortly after. I knew Daren's parents were religious, but I was surprised Misty picked up on it the way that she did.

I stared at the empty plate in front of me, the awkwardness of the situation was almost too much to bear.

"I'm going to fix myself a plate and head upstairs," I said to no one directly.

"Great," Misty chimed as silverware clanged on her plate, "Hide away in your room as you always—"

Daren cut her off. "Misty!" He looked at her with a knowing glance, like they had discussed something without me. It was always about the same thing when people got to my age. I fixed my plate with a little bit of everything, before heading upstairs. I could hear

Michael's parents discussing something as I left the table.

Upstairs, I shut myself in my room. I placed my plate on my desk and turned on my TV. I liked to keep updated on what was going on in the world. But as I turned the TV on, I had a cold rush of sadness in my heart. It wasn't going to matter what happened, in a week, two weeks, or a hundred. I would be gone. I blocked the foreboding feeling in my heart and shook my head.

I looked at my food. The colors of the food on my plate made me feel a nostalgia I hadn't felt in a long time. I tried a little bit of everything, the taste of it was fair, nothing to write home about, but that was to be expected from store brand pre-made meals.

I stayed up in my room either doing research or panicking about the end of my life that was slowly encroaching. It felt as if there was a constant battle to clear the negative thoughts in my mind. The TV flashed a bunch of colors and chimed like there was an important news announcement.

"It was a beautiful day today on April 14th, 2090. That is, until some recent news. For those who missed it, today's top story! President Magdin has approved the use of cyber implants in children, which is criticized by his opponents as completely unnecessary and should wait till they're more developed." A quick segment of a speech by our president then appears on the screen. The tall, dark man speaks to a room of press reporters.

"One question at a time, please," the president said to the room in a cool manner.

"Mr. President!" a young reporter said. "What has led you to approve such a gross and unnecessary technology for children? Are you not aware of the risks it poses for their development?"

"I'm aware of the risks, but there are also benefits that can be discussed between the parents. This is by no means mandatory, and I'm simply allowing the medical field to use this technology to improve the lives of children who would greatly benefit from cybernetic implants." I pressed the power button to turn the TV off. Did these people forget what happened fifty-odd years ago? John Done nearly wiped out our civilization. And now? If he was still around? Let's just give him a direct connection to our children.

I sighed deeply, fearing for this nation's future. I finished what little food I have left on my plate and placed it outside of my door on the floor. I didn't wish to see them, and I figured they didn't wish to see me. I closed the door behind me as I spoke a command, "Night mode."

The lights that rimmed the ceiling above me dimmed to a lower, more tolerable brightness. I slowly inched my way into bed. Once I'm inside the bed, it reclines to a perfect position that it recognizes to be the most comfortable for my body type. The sound of the ocean and ships creaking surrounded me as my nighttime settings took effect. A dark blue hue took over the room. After a few micro adjustments to my bed settings, my aching body finally relaxed into place.

As I completed my nightly routine, I stared at the ceiling for several minutes. Pondering nothing important. Lightning flashed as projections of waves crashed against either side of me. A looming dread in my chest slowly built more and more every day. If I could just get this over with, maybe the world would be a better place.

6

A retro alarm blared into my dreams, interrupting a conversation I longed to have every night.

"Alarm off," I said in a groggy voice. I reached for my bedside water that was there perpetually. I did my morning stretches to prevent cramping and I walked over to my computer once I was finished. I took a seat, leaned back, and stared at the ceiling. The cosmic stars shifted as galaxies danced in one another. This was a live display of what was happening in our galaxy. This turned on automatically at around six a.m. This display always made me feel so small, but it would always help motivate me to do what I wanted.

I switched the display to a dark stormy night. With how the light reflected from the ceiling, it made it seem like it was raining within my bedroom. A forest surrounded me, and the quiet chirps of forest creatures comforted me deeply. Of course, it wasn't real, it was just an illusion. The noise helped me focus, it was like someone would flip a switch within my head and turn off all the noise once the rain started to fall.

After a few moments I stood up and looked inside my personal fridge. I grab a Nutria and sat back down. Once I was comfortable I slid the flavorful mush into my mouth. This particular flavor was stir-fry chicken and noodles, underrated in my opinion. The second the contents entered my mouth I got this rush of flavor. First the seasoned chicken, the texture wasn't there, but that flavor was unmistakable. When that finishes, the seasoning of the sauces and noodles mixed it, adding such depth of flavor. Onion, garlic, soy sauce, sesame, chili. It was so delicious.

"Hey, Cassandra!" A loud voice echoed through the rainy forest. I tried to ignore her but was unsuccessful. I turned to see my daughter Misty standing there with an annoyed expression on her face.

"Yes, my dear?" I said in a polite tone.

"I'm going out with Daren, make sure Michael does his homework and cleans the kitchen," Misty said, matter-of-factly.

"Of course, don't worry. I'll lead the role in which you live to push onto others," I said, without a misstep.

Wordlessly, Misty sneered and slammed my door. A sense of longing crept below my breast, and I sighed.

"Well, guess I should start my day," I said to no one at all. I had developed a bit of a bad habit of talking to myself. I had this hope that if I speak into the void, someone might answer back. Bring me company. Maybe if I did or said enough, I would feel better. Yet, that is not my reality. I'm alone and miserable. Sighs sporadically littered my inner dialogue to no one.

I turned on my TV that was perpetually on the news channel. It felt cliché, but I was an oldy who loved the news. Hopefully they had something more positive today. I didn't remember when exactly, but the news usually stopped reporting every little bad thing that happened in our country. It was mostly positive all the time unless some rare tragedy or major news event occurred somewhere in the world. A beautiful blonde woman spoke as my attention focused on the television.

"Another year and another low crime record! Isn't that amazing, Jim?" the reporter said with a perfect smile, looking toward her co-host.

"Yes, you're right, Janet! Twenty-four percent crime rate per one million citizens in our beautiful U. S. of A.! Isn't that just remarkable? Don't you remember when they changed the statistic from a hundred thousand to a million?" said Jim in his sultry radio voice.

"I do! What a time to be alive in America. In new, news—" Janet paused. "Don't you just love that? New news! So fun! Anyway..."

I cringed at her dialogue.

"Congress has rejected the proposal from the Free-Thinkers party to create humanoid-robots for factory positions!" Janet said.

"Wow! Those Free-Thinkers are still on about that? Why do you think that is?" Jim said in an unprofessionally curious tone.

"I'm not sure personally, but this will be more fuel to the fire for those conspiracy theorists that think robots are replacing human workers again," Janet said. I giggled at this remark, this was a very common theory that corporations have fully replaced humans with robots in their factories. No evidence existed of this claim.

"That seems to be another loss for the Free-Thinkers corporate party, there is always better luck next time." Both of the hosts laughed, and I smirked at this remark. Just then I heard a knock at my door. Before I could ask who it was, Michael's standing right next to me.

"What-cha doin', Grandma?" Michael said with remarkably curious eyes.

"Oh, I just turned on the news. Aren't you supposed to be in class?" I asked.

"Nope! Early day, so I came in to bug you! Where's Mommy?"

"I'm not sure, she just said she was going out. Tell you what, is my fridge running out of snacks? Can you check for me?" I pointed to the small personal refrigerator in the corner. Micheal hurried over and touched the screen on the door.

"It says you're low on your favorite Nutrias, and tea!" Michael said. I could then hear the musical chimes of the tapping of the fridge as he fiddled with the touchscreen.

"I guess we can go out then! Want to head to the grocery store and get some snacks?"

"Only if we get *Galaxy Gummies*!" he said in a roar of excitement.

"We'll get Galaxy Gummies!" I said as we held hands, and he jumped ecstatically.

I prepared my things and got ready as Michael waited impatiently downstairs. I could hear him playing his virtual soccer game, an occasional "*Goal!*" from downstairs, followed by the cheering of the simulated crowds.

"I'm ready, let's get going, Michael," I said, reaching out my hand for him. He grabbed mine in a flash and squeezed it a little too tightly again. A bad habit certainly, a little too enthusiastic with his love, which isn't always a bad thing.

We strolled out of the house, hand-in-hand, and walked down the sidewalk towards the bus pick-up point. I opened the city bus app on my phone and sent out a notification that I was at this specific point and ready to be picked up. We only waited two minutes before a bus arrived at our location. Michael   and   I boarded the red bus. I scanned my bus QR code twice, once for myself, and once for Michael. Children rode free, but they just wanted to keep track of the total passengers. As usual, the bus was pretty spotless. The faux-leather material the seats were made of was durable, comfy, and clean. We planted ourselves towards the back and watched as people got on and off the bus. Michael and I played our favorite game.

"What do you think he's thinking?" I whispered. Pointing to the man in a business suit with a stressed look on his face, talking to himself. Michael stopped and thought for a moment then said, "Man! I shouldn't of ate that fourteenth burger!" in a mock, masculine voice. He giggled uncontrollably. I also giggled.

"Fourteen?! That's so many!" I said.

"Yeah! Thats why his face is like that. He's about to poop himself!" We both chuckled quietly in our seats.

"Michael, what about her?" I picked a different woman with a jacket that had LED lights around the trim and collar. She stood a few feet in front of us. She fidgeted with her collar and pants every few moments.

"That vampire got my neck *and* my butt!" He laughed so loudly that she whipped her head around and Michael looked away, pretending he wasn't involved. I pretended to scold him so she would look away, but then gave him a low-five.

"Those butt vampires are dangerous," I said.

"Yeah, they get you when your most vulnerable!" We both laughed. I heard someone speak loudly enough for me to hear.

"Yeah, and my service was out... and then I was like—What is this? The Great Reset," a woman said just on the other side of our seat loud enough for me to hear. She laughed at her own joke. How crass. I didn't think I could ever make light of such a tragedy. I turned my head back and picked another person.

"What about them?" I said, pointing to somebody with a big smile on her face. She had glasses on, probably watching something on her perspective screen.

"My boss kissed my sister! And I'm gonna be rich!" Michael roared in laughter. We both tried to stifle our excitement, but we couldn't. For the rest of the ride, we made remarks towards other passengers and had an amazing time.

Eventually we arrived in the center of Lowile and made our way to the grocery store. It wasn't very far from the bus drop-off point. In the distance I saw that weird woman again. Always yelling about her missing daughter. I pulled Michael to the other side of me, away from her.

"Has anyone seen my daughter? She was kidnapped!" She frantically waved a flier above her head. We got close enough for her to touch us.

"Please! Have you seen my daughter!" she shouted at me, reaching for my arm. I backed away before she could reach me.

"No, I—"

"Here! This is what she looks like! She may look different now, I think, but if you see her, please let me know." She handed me the flier and I took it, hoping this was an easy way out of this awkward situation.

"I'll let you know," I said, to end the conversation.

"Thank you, a thousand times. Thank you," she pleaded, then went back to shouting for more help. I took a brief look at the flier. She was pretty, that woman's daughter.

"Grandma, is that lady back there okay? She looks like she's thinking about nothing," Michael said in an almost scared voice.

"Nothing? Why do you say that?"

"I don't know. But it's scary." I attempted to comfort him by placing my hand on his shoulder.

"It's okay. She just misses her family. Come on. Let's get those Galaxy Gummies." And as if nothing had happened at all, Michael was back to his cheery self.

"*GALAXY GUMMIES!!!*" he shouted, and his walk turned into a joyful skip.

When we arrived at the grocery store, Michael started chanting a mantra of "Gal-axy Gumm-ies, Gal-axy Gumm-ies!" over and over until we picked up the aforementioned fruity snacks.

"Grandma! Its flavor is out of this *world!*" Michael said, nearly shaking with excitement. I was not so impressed with that unoriginal tagline, but it brought him joy, so I acknowledged him.

"What?! No way! That is so cool. I'll have to try some." As if we hadn't had this conversation several times before.

Next, we picked up some tea that I liked. Earl Grey. Pretty much the same as it was when I was a kid. Just add a little bit of milk and sugar. Amazing.

"Grandma. Tea is gross," Michael said, making a stink face at my choice of drink.

"Not as gross as you! *Ohhh!*" I said, Michael just stared at me. Unimpressed with my insult. "That killed, back in the day."

"Did it?" Michael said.

"No," I said, smiling. We continued our shopping trip until we reached the Nutrias.

"Are there any flavors you like?" I said, pointing to the Nutrias.

"Chicken and waffles!" he answered immediately.

"Oh yeah? That sounds good." I reached for one of the boxes.

"That's the small one, get the twenty pack, it's bigger value! We love value, Grandma!" he said, picking up the larger box.

"That won't be necessary, I—" but I stopped myself. He didn't need to know yet. He gave me a puzzled look.

"You're right. Let's get the bigger one."

"Grandma," he said with sincerity.

"Yes, dear?"

"It looks like you're thinking about something that is sad," he said. This was accompanied by a look I had not seen in a while from any person I knew. Then I remembered what it was... concern. I smiled sweetly at him and tussled his hair and continued our shopping, picking up a few more items for the family.

We arrived at the checkout lane, where I was greeted by a kind worker, who scanned my items. I held up my watch to the payment device and it approved the transaction. They put the items in a Blastic bag, the "better plastic", even though the bag wasn't plastic at all.

"Thank you for all that you do," the worker said to me. This confused me.

"I'm sorry?" I asked.

"For your service. Without the sacrifice of our elders, the world would be in a horrible place. Thank you," the worker said, sounding genuine in their gratefulness. I was put off by her comment, but I thanked them, nonetheless. Michael seemed to not notice and helped me carry our spoils, even insisting he carried the heavier bags.

"Grandma, you gotta let the man carry the heavy stuff," he said, clearly struggling with the contents.

"Now who taught you that old way of thinking?" I asked Michael as we exited the grocery store and headed towards the clean sidewalks.

"Well, Dad said that if you are the man, you gotta do all the heavy lifting and provide for the family," Michael said, nearly dragging the bag on the ground. I got on one knee, making eye contact with Michael, and thought about what I should say before I spoke.

"Michael, honey. Did Daren tell you that? You can't put that pressure on someone. It isn't healthy. We work together, as a unit. Making up for each other's weaknesses. That is what a real man would do," I said as I switched our bags so that he had the lighter one.

"Isn't that more comfortable for you?" I said to him, and he nodded but looked mournful.

"Sorry, Grandma. I just thought I should help you because you're getting older and—"

"Now stop right there, young man. Just because I'm getting old, doesn't mean you should treat me differently. Treat me as you always have. That is what I love about you." I stopped for a moment and kissed his forehead. "Now, let's go home."

We waited at the bus stop for less than a minute before another bus pulled up. This one was one of the newer models, much more advanced than the one we were just on. Using my watch this time, I scanned us both before finding our seats.

These seats were much more comfortable than the normal seats. They reminded me of first-class airliner seats. They had a TV in front of each connecting seat, with two to three seats per side. These TVs played nearly any free show or movie. But if you wanted to you could sync your phone and play a streaming service you were subscribed to. The public transportation system really had improved in the past few years. My favorite part was on your device, you would enter your desired destination. When the bus got close to your stop, it would notify you, so you wouldn't miss it.

We arrived at our stop and walked back home, where we noticed his dad's truck in my driveway. Only the worst of the worst people still own a gas-powered vehicle, especially those who owned trucks but did nothing with them. No construction. No delivery. They just owned a gas guzzling powered vehicle to pollute our planet. I got a feeling of dread as I knew what was about to happen.

I walked to the door and grabbed the handle, but I hesitated. I breathed in deeply and walked inside. Daren and Misty were in my living room, already looking upset.

"Where were you?" Misty said, as if I was a teenager caught coming home late from a party.

"Sorry, Mom," I said in a sarcastic tone, "I was getting some groceries for the week and spending quality time with my grandson, I hope that isn't too much to ask." Misty stared blankly, avoiding my gaze and looked down at Michael.

"You're in trouble, young man, why didn't you text me that you were going out? Why didn't you clean the kitchen like I asked?" Misty glared at me, "You couldn't tell him either? You can't fucking do anything right." Daren put his hand on Misty as if she shouldn't curse with Michael in the room. "I'll say whatever I want, Daren. Let go of me."

This whole time it felt like I was having an out of body experience. I didn't ask these people to live with me. They were irresponsible with their money, so they lost their house. Now? They treated me like trash because they knew I wouldn't kick them out because of Michael.

"I'll do the dishes," I said, turning away from them. I placed my hand on Michael who had been standing by my side the entire conversation. "Go upstairs and do what you like, this isn't your responsibility."

"Don't tell him what to do. Need I remind you? *I* am the mother here. What? *Now* you want to start raising children?" I felt a burning deep in my chest but said nothing.

I walked over to the sink, where there was a slew of dirty dishes, none of which I had created, except one. Michael had a hand in the mess, but he didn't create a majority of these. I cleaned them off and put them in the dishwasher and started a load. Taking a total of five minutes out of my day. I walked past and heard Misty and Daren talking quietly to one another.

"Don't worry, Daren. We have peace of mind knowing she has booked her Endo appointment. She's as good as dead," Misty snickered as I listened from the other end of the wall.

"Great, are we still going to move to China when we get the money?" Daren asked, as if he had no clue.

"Yes. We are going to sell this Alleghany and start a new life overseas. It'll be just like how we dreamed when we were younger."

"I can still take my truck?" Daren asked, stupidly.

"Of course, dear," they said, and I then heard them making out on *my* furniture. I gagged in my mind and loudly walked upstairs, stomping as hard as my body would let me. Alleghany? Really, Misty? You don't know the first thing of those times.

"Grandma?" I heard a quiet voice to my left.

"Yes, Michael, my dear?"

"Why do they treat you like that?" Michael said behind the door to what used to be my fathers' room.

"That is something I would like to know. Don't you mind that, Michael, you go enjoy your games. I've got to get some work done. Alright? We can hang out tomorrow if you'd like," I said, not even looking in his direction.

I went to close the door to my room, trying to put that unpleasant interaction behind me. When I heard hurried footsteps, I figured it was just Velen, trying to find a moment to sneak around when no one was out. I peeked out from inside my room at who might be creeping around, when I saw the back of Michael's head. He nearly sprinted down the steps. He was probably hungry and going to get some sna—

"Apologize to Grandma, right now!"

A small voice, clearly not used to being raised, came from the ground floor. I was in utter shock. I hadn't had many people come to my defense before, let alone my grandchild to his mother. I left my quarters and peeked down the steps, but Michael was around the corner having the discussion out of sight.

"What did you just say to me?" Misty snapped, nearly twice as loud. Michael didn't lower his voice.

"Why are you so mean to Grandma?! She does everything for us. She does everything you ask!"

Michael sounded strained from the few words he had shouted.

"Michael Bennet Moore! You do *not* talk to us that way!"

"Why? You only talk to Grandma and me this way. Saying meanie things." By this point, I was almost down the stairs.

"Michael, Dear. I don't talk to anyone in a mean way, they simply—"

"Yes you do! You always get mad for no reason and make Grandma feel bad!" The sadness in his voice broke me. Even though he was so young, nine years old, he could perfectly understand the situation I was in.

Then I heard the sound of stomping on a wooden floor, followed by the unmistakable noise of a hand meeting a face.

"Misty! What the hell?" Daren shouted. "Don't leave any bruises or we could be in deep shit!"

"He needs to be put in his place. He needs to realize he'll *never* talk to me like that." By this point I was already down the stairs, no longer trying to hide my presence.

"Why are you so mean to everyone!" Michael shrilled; tears streamed down his face. He didn't acknowledge me as he ran past, up the stairs and slammed his door. My fury was unbridled.

"Really? That's how we are going to respond to a child asking, 'Why are you guys mean?' More violence?" Misty looked away from my words, fists clenched.

"Like you know anything about being a parent," Misty said in a hushed tone, facing away from me.

"I'm quite aware of how to be a parent, are you open for private lessons to teach me how to become one? Because that was some grade A parenting right there. What more do you want from me, Misty?" I asked, genuinely curious at what she might say.

Before she responded, Daren interjected. "Don't talk to her like that!" He stood up and immediately tried to intimidate me with his size. Although he was nearly a foot taller than me, I wasn't scared of him.

"Like how, Daren? Like a person who just hit a child? I have done nothing but try to communicate over the years. You never reach out; you never want to come over. Suddenly, when I'm about to die, you want to live here and 'help out'." I air-quoted with my fingers.

"You're pathetic. You've never done anything worth a damn in your entire life. Thats why your husband left you," Daren said. I was admittedly shocked by the accusation.

"You don't know a goddamn thing about my husband," I said through gritted teeth.

"Couldn't have liked you that much. Didn't he suddenly leave one day when you were out of town? Two kids by yourself?" Daren said.

"Shut up, Daren!" I said with unchecked hostility. "If Misty told you that, then you know what really happened. Don't put that on me. I don't dig up *your* past."

"Because you don't know the first thing about me, Cassy. You just sit in your room all day, wasting away. I bet you're so excited for your Endo appointment," Daren sneered. I just wanted to punch that smile off his face.

"I'm not wasting away, if you were ever around, you would know that I'm out quite frequently in the morning. You just come home drunk. You're probably cheating on your wife." I looked towards Misty. I didn't know why I said that, nor why I looked at her.

"You would know a lot about that, right? What was it again? Didn't you sleep with some guy in Chicago while your dad was dying in the room next to you?" How did he know that? I was utterly appalled at his knowledge of my past.

"Daren, honey..." Misty said, realizing the situation may have escalated too far.

"And that room you love so much? Don't worry, once you're dead, it's gone. Along with this whole house. The only memory anyone here will have of you is the image of you staring at a computer screen," Daren said, staring down at me.

What made me maddest about this situation was that I didn't get to him. His stare told me how little he thought of me. I had done things he could never even dream of accomplishing. I wanted to say more, but I lacked the foresight in seeing the point.

There was only an utter silence remaining. I turned around and left the room and this conversation behind me. I entered my room without looking back, closed the door behind me and lay up against it. Sliding down its surface until I reached the floor. I wept silently.

The weeping turned into a tornado of hysteria as I tried to catch my breath, but I was unable. I crawled my way to my bed, but I felt a panic attack creeping at the edges of my body. I was extremely dizzy and weak. I couldn't breathe. I started gasping for air like I had been kicked in the stomach. The door started creaking, and I feared my daughter or her husband will come to pour salt on my wounds, but it was neither.

"Grandma… I want to…" he said before entering the room fully. "*Grandma!*" Michael ran over to me and held me tightly, too tightly as always, I was nearly losing consciousness. The room's lights seemed to flicker. My vision doubled and I swore I saw a shadow figure looking down from the projection screen above me.

171

The sliding doors to my doctor's office opened before me. I was hit by a pleasant smell, as I had grown accustomed. I immediately approached the front desk where I was greeted by the receptionist.

"Mrs. Moore! How are you feeling today?" Sharon asked. She sounded genuinely curious.

"I'm pretty grateful. I have my family here. Going to set up the big appointment," I said with the warmest smile I could muster.

"Wow! Okay! That is wonderful. Well, the doctor is currently tending to a few patients, but if you want to sit over there..." She pointed to some unoccupied chairs in the corner. "He'll be with you shortly."

I nodded and smiled sweetly towards her before finding my seat.

"How long is this going to take?" I heard Daren whisper to Misty.

"Shouldn't be too long." Misty shrugged. "What, they probably do a quick check up, ask a few questions. Shouldn't be more than an hour."

Daren audibly groaned before pulling out his perspective glasses that he used to watch streaming services privately. Misty did the same as I just sat contently. It was nice seeing them. It had been so long since I saw them last. Although, I think we had a big fight after Michael's eighth birthday party. I missed that boy; he was so kind to me and so excited about learning. I wondered what he wanted to be when he grew up.

After a few moments of sitting, Daren looked impatient and stood up and walked to the front desk. I saw him chatting with the receptionist. She giggled every now and again, and Daren had this smug look about him. I rolled my eyes and glanced toward Misty. She seemed not to notice, or maybe she was pretending not to.

"Cassandra Moore?" A nurse looked around, waiting for someone to respond.

"Here I am, I'm coming." I said this in a crotchety way, although I didn't mean it to come out as such.

The nurse checked my temperature as my daughter and her husband stood by. We were led to a room in the back, and I found my seat on an exam table. Misty and her husband took a seat nearby.

"Alright! You're here to set up your Endo appointment today, Mrs. Moore? Is that right?" the woman asked.

"Yes, that is correct," I said to her.

"Oh! And I see you brought your family with you today. I haven't met you two before! What are your names?"

"Daren, it's my pleasure to meet you," Daren said, with doe eyes.

"Misty, I'm Cassandra's daughter." Misty paused. "You have beautiful hair, what conditioner do you use?"

The nurse looked flattered as she bobbed her hair. "This? Oh, I go to the salon, they have those machines where you put your hair in it, and it comes out silky smooth every time! Magic I tell you." The nurse clearly looked giddy that someone had noticed.

"And your tattoos are so cool!" Daren said, inspecting her arm and gently touching her. "They glow neon in the light! So awesome!" I rolled my eyes. Now I remembered why I didn't go anywhere with them. They did this every time. Like they had something to prove to every person that they were just the best people in the world. After their conversation the nurse returned to the reason I was here today.

"Let me just check your vitals really quickly. Any changes since we last saw you?" she said, typing and talking towards a holographic keyboard and display on the wall.

"Nope. Same as I always been," I said. The nurse looked hurried as she checked my vitals, inside my ears, then listened to my heartbeat.

"Any neurological implants since we last met?" I shook my head no. "All seems normal then. The doctor will be in to perform the psych evaluation and Endo test. It was wonderful meeting you two!" she said as she exited the room. Misty and Daren both chimed in agreement as the nurse left.

"Psych evaluation?" Daren asked Misty.

"Yeah, they have to make sure you're doing this of your own accord." Misty looked at me expectantly. I wished she would at least be a little subtle. "If they suspect she's being pressured in any way, they cancel the appointment and all future attempts at participating."

"Wow. I didn't know it was that serious," Daren said. Misty nodded.

"That is why it's very important that we do it right the first time," she said, crossing her arms as she looked at me.

I pretended they weren't here. I didn't even know why I was excited to have them here in the first place. I guessed a small part of me was hoping that this would be a nice experience, but what was I thinking? I was signing my life away. How could this have been a nice experience? The doctor finally entered the room, with a folder in hand.

"Hello. I'm Dr. Garcia. I'll be performing the psych evaluation for Endo today. How are you today, Mrs. Moore?"

"Perfectly fine, thank you."

"This is your family, I'm assuming," he said, pointing towards the couple. I nodded.

"Alright. For this part, you two will have to be in a separate room, please wait outside for now." Daren looked shocked, but Misty expected this. They both exited the room. The doctor folded out a table and handed me a thin tablet.

"I'll ask you some questions when you finish, but for now, answer honestly and to the best of your ability. I'll also be taking any cellular device or technological equivalent and placing them to the side while we do your assessment."

I complied and gave him my phone and watch; not like I used them much anyways.

I looked at the tablet and pulled out the stylus from the top of the tablet. A white screen appeared with a single question.

What is your full legal name?

I paused and wrote "Cassandra Lilith Moore". Then I pressed the next question.

What is the name of the city and state that you are currently living in?

Lowile, Nebraska.

What is 2+2?

This caused me to hesitate. Not because the answer was difficult, quite the opposite in fact. It was the subject matter of the question. Was this all that was required to participate in the End of Life program? I answered four.

Where are you located, currently?

I answered "the doctor's office". I almost put a question mark after my answer but thought better of it.

Are there any ailments that are the reason for your willingness to participate in the End of Life Program? Please answer specifically below.

I held the tablet firmly. I stared down at its screen, contemplating the words before me. I penned "none" down before proceeding to the next question.

Do you feel as though you have been pressured by a family member or any other person to participate in the End of Life Program? Please answer honestly.

Again, I hesitated. I selected "No".

Would you be willing to be an organ doner after completing your willful participation in the End of Life Program?

I wrote "yes".

By signing this document at the bottom, you are acknowledging that you agree and by your own volition are participating in the End of Life Program. Thereby ending your life through the process of euthanasia. This is a painless procedure and can be stopped until injection. Once the procedure has started, there is no means of reversal.

I signed and dated at the bottom and pressed continue.

Do you understand that the funds go directly to your children or spouse and not any other living family members?

Unless you have no children or spouse, in which case the money can either be withdrawn or donated to a charity of your choice. The $50,000 donation can also be put into a savings account with a fixed 5.0% APY which can only be recovered by a living spouse/child 5 years after your participation in the End of Life Program. For further explanation, you can ask your healthcare provider. Please select which form of donation you would like to provide.

- *No Donation*
- *Charity*
- *Direct Deposit to Child/Spouse*
- *5-Year Plan*

I selected direct deposit, since I was going to be dead, and it didn't really matter to me. I signed my name and the date.

Thank you for your participation in the End of Life Program! Your dedication to a better future for the entire world will not be forgotten.

I passed the doctor the tablet, signifying I was finished. I knew they'd streamlined the process a few years ago, but I didn't think it would be that easy to sign up for the End of Life program. The doctor tapped a few buttons on the tablet before speaking to me.

"Everything looks good here, Mrs. Moore. And are you sure about your willingness to participate? You can withdraw at any point." I sighed; this was getting a bit excessive. I get it, I can pull out of the program at any time.

"Yes. I am completely sure," I said firmly.

"Perfect. I'll go retrieve your family and you'll be free to go, is there any facility you would like to go to specifically?" he asked.

I hadn't thought about it. I had no idea how to answer him.

"Whatever facility is closest will be fine."

"Perfect, we'll set you up with the one here in Lowile. We'll be sending out a detailed email of the preparations you need to complete before your appointment." The doctor looked kind and thoughtful as he spoke. Completely contrasting how Misty and Daren treated me.

"That sounds perfect. I appreciate your time, doctor."

"Anytime. Thank you, Cassandra. It was a pleasure getting to know you over the years." He reached out for a hug; I complied and held him closely. For some reason, his shoulder felt wet. But it wasn't his shoulder that was leaking, it was my face. "Is everything alright?" he asked, pulling me away.

"Ah, it's just… It feels real now. Like this is it. It feels like this has been looming over me for several years now, but now it's finally here." I coughed into my elbow; my emotions were a little unsteady.

"Trust me when I say, you're not my first patient to feel this way. You know, if it wasn't for the Endo, our world wouldn't be as it is now." He grabbed my hand. "Thank you, Cassandra. Your sacrifice doesn't go unnoticed."

This made my heart swell then calm. Dr. Garcia showed me out of the room and led me back to my family who were now waiting in the reception area. Misty smiled at me, and we made our way out of the office.

"So, we can't give you a ride. We have some, uh—" Daren looked at Misty. "Stuff to do."

"That is fine. You didn't drive me here; I didn't expect you to drive me back."

"Well… That's cool. I guess. We'll see you 'round," Daren said.

"I guess you will. I love you two." But they were already gone, making their way back to his white truck. I walked alone on that chilly, sunny afternoon to the nearest bus stop.

5

The bus bumped along as I stared out the window.

"You have that look again, Grandma," Michael said next to me.

"Don't mind me, I'm just thinking."

"What are you thinking about? Wait, no… let me guess! You're thinking about all the fun we are going to have at Rat City!" He said.

"No… well yes. I'm thinking about how much I love you! Are you excited?" I asked.

"*So* excited! I've never been to the Rat City before!" Michael said.

"Neither have I! It'll be a nice experience for us both," I said as we sat waiting to arrive at our stop that so happened to be right outside Rat City. The building had a scruffy-looking rat with red eyes as its mascot. It was creepy and cute at the same time. I didn't know why people went here.

Rat City, really, was just an arcade with a lot of "5D" reality warping technology that the average consumer couldn't afford. A majority of the booths had self-cleaning VR headsets where you entered a pod and experienced an adventure such as fighting dinosaurs or traveling through space. It was what I expected from a modern arcade. I found myself in the adult section which was a bar with rat memorabilia everywhere. I kept Michael within my vision as I watched him play. I turned to order something when I noticed the bartender, a beautiful woman with long hair.

"You look familiar," I said to the woman at the bar.

"Are you trying to hit on me? You're a little too old for me, sweetie," she said.

I laughed boisterously. "No, no. I wouldn't do that. I've seen you somewhere, but I can't quite place it." The woman stopped wiping the counter, and looked a little more serious.

"Probably my mother. Are you aware of a lady that stands around town and waves a missing persons flier?"

"Is that where I know you from?"

"Most likely." She sighed. "My mother has late-stage dementia. A cure for it is a chip they put in your brain to help increase stimulation using a specific set of frequencies. It's supposed to help stimulate the parts of the brain that aren't producing the chemicals and hormones that they should be."

"Yes, and?" This conversation brought me back to my interviewing days.

"Well, it made her have intense delusions and she forgets I exist even though we live with each other. Sometimes she even sees me when I'm not there. Most of the time though, if I'm not in her direct vision, she believes I'm either missing or kidnapped."

"That is awful!"

"It's very heartbreaking. The implant was supposed to make her better, but as you can tell, she is not."

"Why is that?"

"Rare chance. You know when you go to the doctor, and they say there is a 'very small chance' something bad will happen? Well, that 'very small chance' happened to her."

"Anything they can do?"

"Not really. Once you put in the chip, it's really difficult to take out without damaging the brain or causing another issue. So, they usually just leave it in there."

"That is really sad. I had no idea you were the 'crazy corner lady's' daughter."

"That's what people call her? Makes sense. I wish there was something I could do. I just come home, and she's happy to see me, like she hasn't been out all day announcing my kidnapping. Then I go to work, she boards a bus, heads downtown, and posts flyers of me saying, 'Missing' or 'Help'."

"Thank you for telling me this. I always thought it was strange no one would help her."

"Yeah. Unfortunately, there is nothing to be done really. I did read something concerning online though."

"What's that?"

"That people are able to hack the neurochips people put in your brain and cause your brain to think and see things it isn't supposed to."

"Like what?"

"I read somewhere that this person's dad got an implant after a work accident. He lost his memories, and the implant was supposed to restore the memories he lost."

"Yeah."

"Well. Apparently, it gave him false memories and he started knowing things he couldn't have possibly known."

"Like what?"

"He was fluent in Italian, even though he was a Mid-westerner like us with no family roots to Italy. He could also remember living in the vineyards of Italy, even when he had never gone there. Totally destroyed the family because the dad didn't know them anymore. Had no connection to them whatsoever."

"Do you think something like that is happening to your mother?"

"No idea. But that isn't even the craziest part of the story. The man died shortly after, too many complications. When they looked inside of his head for the chip, it was apparently one that was refurbished and was already in someone else's head before."

"That's… interesting."

"Dystopian you mean? It was the equivalent to total mind control. The person who posted the story said that he had to sign an NDA, and wasn't allowed to talk about it, but it seems he did."

"What has that to do with hacking of the chips though?"

"Oh, sorry. It turns out that those chips often 'glitch' and people see things or hear things they aren't supposed to. But it's thought that you can gain remote access to someone's brain and make them feel whatever they want, MKUltra style."

"Do you think that is what is happening to your mother?" The woman stopped cleaning up around her and thought hard for a moment.

"What would you like to drink?" I was shocked by the sudden change in conversation.

"A water is fine." She poured water from a machine with a long nozzle and slid the glass in front of me.

"To answer your question, I feel it's certainly more interesting that her brain is being hacked, then simply being the 'crazy corner lady'. I'm just glad she's turning eighty soon."

I lost my breath for a second. "Why is that?"

"Oh, so that I don't have to take care of her anymore. That she can participate in the Endo and be dead and this will all be behind me. Maybe I'll go to Hawaii, or what's left of it." I was suddenly no longer interested in this conversation. I had a horrible feeling deep in the pit of my stomach.

"Thank you for the drink."

4

"That is my story. I hope you enjoyed it," said an elderly gentleman as his closing remarks to his submission to the End of Life program's website. It was a decent story, he fought in the Water Wars which was a brief conflict that was forgotten about once the Reset happened.

He had never experienced combat on the front lines, but he was defending an aquifer in Africa from locals and never saw much action. It was interesting, but rather dull as he wasn't a very good storyteller. My story hadn't gotten many views yet. But I imagine some people may find it interesting.

I removed my headphones and aimed to get some Nutrias from my fridge, but it was suspiciously empty. I knew I shouldn't have gotten Michael's favorite flavor.

I left my room and opened the door to what was temporarily Michael's room to see if he was in there. It was empty, besides all the new high-tech equipment I knew he wanted. Not only did he have a VR headset and immersive system downstairs, but a full-blown VR station upstairs as well. Incredibly expensive, but no expense was too small for Michael. It was a little pod with a built in omni-directional movement for real life transmission of movement. The VR headset was incredibly comfortable and was supported by a docking station that connected to the headset. The headset could transmit in-game smells and the audio was some of the best on the market. It was like being transmitted into video games for real. The technology at Rat City was very comparable and I bet he would've been a little disappointed by the lack of improvement from what he had at home.

I then stared at my father's work. The art had faded slightly with time. The portraits, even after all these years, hadn't lost their beauty. I smiled, remembering the man he was, I was very glad he'd left me with this part of who he was. I shut the door and continued downstairs.

"Any day now she'll be dead, and we can leave and do what we've always wanted," Daren said, in a not-so-whisper. I walked in unapologetically to cut their conversation short.

"There is no rush, my dear, you'll get your wishes soon enough." My words surprised him, and Daren almost looked embarrassed, but Misty remained unflinching.

"Finally left your cave, have you?" Misty asked as if she didn't know how much that irritated me.

"Yes, finally done fantasizing about my death?" I asked, walking to the fridge.

"Never," Misty said. I felt as though this conversation wasn't worth my time and I grabbed some Nutrias from the fridge and began to head back upstairs.

Later that night, I tossed and turned. I narrowly avoided a panic attack by practicing my breathing exercises. But now I was having trouble falling asleep. Suddenly, it felt as though I was falling and barely stabilizing myself right before I hit the ground.

A purple meteor fell from the black sky, exploding at my location, obliterating me instantly. Then I rematerialized. I'm instantly run over by a sedan. Next I was drowning, looking towards the glossy surface as hands grabbed at my feet. Skulls surrounded me and piled in a wave that crashed into my body violently. I fell into pieces like shattered glass.

I knew this was a dream, but I couldn't stop these nightmares. I was fully aware of my state of being but every night they came in different forms. My death, my demise. It was approaching and it felt as though there was a small part within me that wanted to live, while the overwhelming trepidation pushed that feeling down to the gravel and stomped on its head.

This was Endo depression at its worst, I think. Recurring nightmares and fear of dying.

If I held on a little longer I could get where I wanted to be.

A man in a black suit holding a machine gun shot me over and over. Every bullet hole repaired itself as I was stabbed again and again by the ballistics. It felt so real. It hurt so much. Lightning struck me in a field with a single birch tree.

Just a little further.

A towering figure stood in front of me with an axe. I closed my eyes within my dream as my head was separated from my body. I felt a sting, but then I opened my eyes.

I was outside a wooden cottage in a field of green. Scotland, I presumed, I had never been there, but this was what my mind pictured it as. The rolling green hills stretched in every direction, seemingly going on forever. I was alone in this field other than this cottage. I approached the door and reached for the handle, but it opened itself.

I let myself in, but it was empty. It was sparsely furnished and had my computer on a desk against a wall. The wall my desk was against had no windows, while every other wall had plentiful windows. The sunshine seemed to stop short of my computer, but then I notice it wasn't my computer. It was a Lost Web computer, probably one of the dozens I used back in the day.

"I missed you," said a voice. I jumped back and looked around, but no one was there.

"Max?" I asked.

"Yes." He grabbed my shoulder from behind and spun me around, I felt his lips press to mine. Suddenly the lurking ache of my bones was gone, and my hair was fuller. I leaned back and embraced his full body.

"Where have you been?" I asked.

"Waiting for you," he said, spinning me around in a dance as our favorite song started playing.

"I'm sorry I wasn't around back then," I said.

"It's fine. You had great things you wanted to do. I just wasn't a part of it," Max said. The words didn't come out as harsh, but as factual. We both knew he wasn't bitter in his tone, but it still hurt me deeply.

"I would change it if I could go back, Max," I said.

"And what? The world was different because of you. I was a small piece of the puzzle that was Cassandra Moore. I just wish we got married, I like how you pretend we did though," he said, kissing me again as our dance began to slow. "Or watch our kids grow. How are they now?" he asked.

"They're fine. I'm not involved with them much now," I admitted, not liking my answer.

"Do you want to be in their lives?" he asked.

"Yes, I do more than anything, Maxwell, but I feel as though my sins have caught up to me, and this is my burden to bear now," I said.

"Cassandra." He embraced me. "You don't have to be so hard on yourself. It's never too late to reconcile. If I was there tomorrow, would you apologize to me? For all the nights you stayed alone in that room? For all the nights you neglected our children?" he asked, again not being harsh, but being honest.

"Without a moment of hesitation," I said.

"Then go do it. Apologize to them, Cassandra. There is still a little time left." And then the dream was over.

3

"He's thinking about how he wants his dog to hurry up, it's cold outside!" Michael said.

"Or are you thinking that Michael?" I asked, sincerely.

"It's a little chilly, why do we get ice cream when it's cold out?"

"So, it doesn't melt!" I shouted, waving my waffle cone in the air. "If you get ice cream on a hot day, you lose so much of it to the heat. It drips all over your hand, then your hand gets sticky. Often, you don't have too many napkins with you. It becomes a terrible inconvenience. That is why you get ice cream when it's cold out," I said, realizing I might sound a little crazy. Michael wordlessly licked his triple cookie chocolate chip.

"It makes sense, I guess," Michael finally said.

"Are you okay?" I asked him.

"It's such a nice day out, besides being cold." He licked his ice cream cone a dozen times before continuing. "It feels like you're hiding something from me, Grandma."

"Why do you say that?" I asked.

"Because it feels like you're thinking about something sad. You have been for a while now. Something you don't want to talk about, but you really want to talk about it. Every time you stare you get this look that confuses me. I don't like it," Michael said.

This confession brought back déjà vu for me; back to the grocery store. I didn't know if I should tell him that

I was participating in the End of Life program soon. He would find out after either way, and I didn't want our final days to be him worrying about my wellbeing. I had lived long enough, I just wanted to enjoy what time I had left with my grandson, unimpeded.

"You worry a lot, Michael. I appreciate you caring about me, but it's nothing for you to put your mind's real estate towards," I said.

The birds sang as we swung our feet on the swings. Children played all around us, some around Michael's age, but he always acted far older than he was. The path we took to get here was cobblestone of all lustrous and interesting rocks. The canopy that enclosed this park left a circular gap for sunshine to pierce through. It was a little-known playground area in Lowile that I liked to come to every now and again.

"Are you going to die?" Michael asked. I coughed at this sudden question. Nearly dropping my mint chocolate chip.

"How? I mean, why? Why would you ask that question?" I asked.

"I have a feeling. My feelings aren't usually wrong. Between you and Mommy, someone is hiding something," Michael said. What a detective he had become, although Misty's lust for my demise wasn't exactly a secret.

"Your mother and I… don't get along. She may say some things that aren't true, but they're hurtful. But that doesn't mean she doesn't love me, and I don't love her," I said.

"Mom saying 'I can't wait for her to die so we can leave this place forever' doesn't mean anything?" Michael asked in a tone which was genuine curiosity and not sarcasm, which I wasn't used to from this family. I chose my next words carefully.

"Your Mother, Misty, has a very odd way of showing affection." I started to sweat a little. "Like she means one thing but says another. I hope in my heart of hearts she doesn't want me to perish, but I'm not her so there is no way for me to know."

"You're turning eighty soon, right, Grandma?" Michael said, ignoring my words as he stared blankly ahead. These words made me sweat even more as I felt the walls closing around me.

"Yes. You remembered! More than most can say."

"Isn't there this… thing people do when they turn eighty?" I think whether I should lie or not.

"Yes, there is. It's a program where you can… donate yourself to help your family's younger generations succeed further," I said, trying to market the End of Life program as anything but pure insanity.

"Do you die when you do it?" Michael asked.

"Yes," I said.

"Promise me something, Grandma," Michael said.

"What is that, my dear?" I said, my guard now fully up.

"That you won't do anything like that. I need you to stay around."

His words crushed me. "I won't, Michael. Just for you," I said.

Michael smiled, finally easing his intense gaze before running off to play with the few other children who are at the park. I swung my feet and watched them play with each other.

1

"Wake up, sleepy head!" I barely heard through a haze of weak consciousness.

"What? Michael? Is that you?" I asked.

"Of course! We got a big day today; I'm hungry, and I have deemed you worthy of taking me out to lunch!" Michael said.

What time is it? Did I forget to set my alarm?

"Oh, do you now? Well, my liege, where do you propose we go for this lunch you speak of?" I asked.

"I had *not* thought that far!" Michael said. We both laughed. What a wonderful way to wake up.

"Go do me a favor really quick and get me some water, I'll be here. Getting ready for our day," I said to him, sweetly. Michael hurriedly scampered off while I got dressed for the day. Still getting over the initial shock of my nightmares. I wondered if he knew today was my birthday or if he was just overly excited to just to be excited...?

Michael returned shortly and knocked on the door before asking to come in.

"Are you dressed or nakey, Grandma?" Michael asked, almost *too* genuinely.

"It'll be a few moments, just wait out there," I said towards the door. I then heard footsteps that were too loud to be Michael's. He made a surprised noise before my door nearly flew off its hinges.

"You going out?" Misty said, hand at her side, coffee in hand.

"Yes. I'm going to lunch with Michael, is that alright?" I asked, although I didn't care what her answer was.

"Perfect. Can you pick me up a couple things?" She then sent me a text of groceries for me to pick up.

"Sure, I'll see to it," I said and she nodded without another word and left my room. That went a lot better than most of our conversations. "Well, I'm finished and ready to go, what about you, Michael?"

"Ready as I'll ever be!" he said, nearly bursting through my door.

We made our way out and down to the bus stop where it was a short ride to Lowile.

Michael and I had a nice lunch at a hot dog stand. The man selling the hot dogs was always nice and fourteen bucks for a hot dog wasn't bad in this economy.

We then went to the grocery store, and picked up the items Misty had asked for, just a bunch of random stuff that I didn't know she used. But if I could be useful on my birthday *and* stay away from her? A win-win if you asked me.

We finished our shopping and I debated whether or not we should stall and hang out longer, but then Michael said, "Mommy says we need to hurry home, I have homework to do," with almost a frown.

"Okay." I frowned at this discovery. "I guess we shouldn't poke the bear."

We changed direction and headed to the bus stop. We were home shortly after. The driveway was empty when we approached my house, which was a relief. Maybe have some peace and quiet tonight on my—

"Surprise!!! Happy eightieth birthday, Cassandra!!!" A loud roar nearly made me have a heart attack. I stumbled backwards as someone grabbed my arm, stabilizing me.

"Oh my! What is this!" The room was filled with my friends, and their friends and my family from out of state. I hadn't talked to these people in ages! Misty hurried up to me and hugged me tightly.

"Happy birthday, Mom," she whispered in my ear. I was totally dumbfounded; I looked down at Michael and he had an evil grin on his face.

"It was my job to distract you while they set up the party!" He hugged my leg, and I patted his head, tears started to well up inside me.

"Thank you for coming, everyone!" I shouted as I pulled away from my daughter and grandchild. "Let's eat some good food and have some drinks!" Everyone cheered and I went to greet my guests. This party was honestly a really nice gesture, and I couldn't believe Misty had set it up for me.

They sang happy birthday to me, we cut some cake, and everyone was a couple of drinks deep. The decorations all around filled my heart with joy as some of my relatives' kids played on the VR headset as Michael showed them how to use it.

I was having a conversation with my good friend, Edith, while she was slurring her words heavily.

"Ya, knows. I don't know whys we don't hang out much anymores. You just calls me on my computer, and like… I don't want to talk. I want to see you." She managed to get out. Clearly far more drunk than I was.

"We should set up something next week, I—" then I stopped myself. I remembered what tomorrow was. "We should see each other soon," I landed on.

"We should! You're a ton of fun, Cassandra! I mished you." I could see she was attempting to give me a hug, I reciprocated, I held her tight. When we pulled apart she stumbled a little backwards. I tried to catch her, but my reflexes weren't as good as they used to be. Her arm slipped through my hand, and she bashed her head on the corner of my table. She fell further and landed on the ground hard. The party fell silent as everyone looked at her. It was like a gunshot had gone off in my kitchen. Blood began to pool behind her head. I screamed as people pushed me out of the way, trying to help.

"Someone call 9-1-1!!!" I heard a voice shout.

It was so red; the blood spread quickly. I had never seen so much blood, not since the Reset. I wordlessly walked away and headed to the hallway bathroom. I locked the door and stared into the mirror. My vision began to double as I felt a panic attack coming on. My legs started shaking as I collapsed to the ground. Tears streamed down my face. I began to hyperventilate.

"The walls are closing," I heard in my head, my own monologue turning against me. I just didn't want to feel anymore. I just wanted this to be over with. No more. No more suffering. Please, God. Let it end.

19,397

When my eyes opened, I looked down. I was in my body but somewhere else. I felt the leather made from shell creatures. It was soft, the textural difference was a shock. The wooden floors I was curled up on were cold, this leather was warm. I looked to my left and noticed my dad was driving an old-world EV. Why was he alive? And young? Where were we? My mouth moved on its own and I suddenly lost all conscious thought.

"Hey, Dad, where did you say you wanted to eat? Brunch somewhere, right? I heard the food's good here in Chicago," I said.

"Yeah, but why don't we let the car's AI decide? Last time it worked well."

"Again? Remember last time in DT Seattle and it took us to that *galactically* sketchy restaurant? Should've went down to Pike's Place and got some—"

"But it was good though, right?" He took his eyes off the road to show me his smirk.

"I concede it was, but I don't know if I want to…" I was startled by an unnatural bump in the car. "Hey Dad, you drunk? You're driving on the sidewalk."

"Huh? No, I'm… What the—?" I could see the effort he was putting into trying to shift the vehicle back towards the road. It wouldn't budge. It began to accelerate.

Without warning the speakers made a horrible screeching noise that caused me to cover my ears. A muffled laughter hid under all of the noise. I stared with my eyes affixed to the sidewalk. Yelling at my father to return to the road. "I'm trying, dammit!"

I stared in horror as three unsuspecting civilians' casual faces turned to looks of shock and fear.

Thud. Thud. Thud. All three went under.

The laughter grew more intense now. I stared in absolute bewilderment and looked to my left, watching several cars collide head on as people were thrown through their windshields. Their bodies sliding across the pavement.

I gazed forward again and screamed. A family with children ran panicked away to attempted safety. I shut my eyes. The car slowed to a crawl as body after body was thrown under us. I felt progressively sicker as the hammering of bones on pavement invaded my eardrums.

Before we could get much further, another EV ran straight into the driver's side of our vehicle. Our car was thrown to the side of a building, stopping us in our tracks. My head whipped around, and I was immediately dizzied.

A cry grabbed my attention. It was my father. There was no one in the EV that rammed us. It backed up and rammed us again. The second time nearly folded the car on my father. His screams were full of agony. He didn't sound like himself; his face went flat and lifeless. My heart raced, and now the thought that my father could be paralyzed entered my brain. I reached for my seatbelt, but the latch was stuck, or wouldn't come undone. The EV rammed thrice now. My father lay unconscious and broken.

0

The doors to the clinic slid open. I was with my daughter, Misty. I told her I wished Michael would not attend this event. She obliged. I wished my last memory with Michael would have been at the hot dog stand and not the party. No one died at least. Poor Edith.

The walls of the clinic that had seemed whimsical and extraordinary at one point now had a dull hue as I walked through the hallways. This place reminded me of that transition in *The Wizard of Oz*, it all seemed so beautiful when you first saw it, but when you know it's coming? The impact is lost.

Misty was surprisingly helpful, doing most of the talking for me. I could hear her voice, but it felt as if my head had separated from my body. I could hear and feel, but the knife plunged deeper with each step. Removing parts of myself. Why was I going through with this anyway?

The iron doors opened, we were sanitized, and then we entered "paradise". Even now the joyful nature of this part of the clinic still had some effect on me, it seemed. My eyes were failing to keep their contents within themselves. I found my seat, but I still didn't think Misty had even spoken to me directly. Her husband owned a vehicle, but the bus ride here was just another afternoon. I felt as though I might be dead any moment. I was overwhelmed by dread. Like before you leap from an airplane, but you're unsure if the parachute will open. Then like fresh scissors to fabric I heard a voice.

"Mr. Garfield?" a very beautiful nurse assistant said. An old man and his, what I was assuming, son slowly helped him up as they walked towards the back. Two people were ahead of me now, it would be any moment.

"Mom." My head whipped in her direction, but I didn't make eye contact. "How are you feeling?" Who had replaced this woman with a replica of my daughter? I struggled to find words; this knocked me out of my momentary dissociation.

"I'm good." I sidestepped in my mind. "I'm okay, it doesn't feel real, ya know?"

"Does everyone have the same feeling I do, sitting next to you?" Misty asked.

"What feeling is that?" I finally looked at her directly.

"Guilt. Lots of guilt." Misty was crying more than I usually did. Snot dribbled out of her nose as she attempted to stifle her emotions. I looked away because this moment was all too confusing for me. I felt like if I kept looking at her I may come to some conclusion that I might not enjoy. I spoke to the open air in front of me.

"It's how I felt, deep down, I suppose. When I was in here with my father."

"You were in here with your father?" Misty asked.

Why did she suddenly want to learn about me now? She had spent many years making my life more difficult than necessary and now she was finding some sort of curiosity within herself.

"Yes, I was. My mother too. They're the reason I got out of the situation I was in all those years ago. Gave me the opportunity to have a half-decent life for you and your brother." I felt the tides of emotion sway within my skull that had been trying to separate itself from this world only moments ago.

"Tell me about her. Your mom," Misty said. I looked over to see her face, expecting to see a malevolent grin. But it was... something. Not what I was used too, especially from her.

"What are you trying to do here?" I asked with a tinge of frustration in my voice.

"I am realizing..." she paused and stuttered, "t-that I may have n-not been the best daughter to you." Her lips trembled. What a great place to have an epiphany, Misty.

"You have had years to contemplate our relationship and your own role within it. You don't get to decide to do so now, moments before I die," I whispered to her.

"Mrs. Riddle?" the same nurse from earlier called out. A woman surrounded by six, no *seven* children all gathered around. Tears in all of their eyes except those of Mrs. Riddle, as they walked towards the backrooms. For some reason, that nurse looked oddly familiar. Of course she did. I had just seen her. My mind was in shambles.

"I was so focused on myself, I think," Misty said. "I tried so hard to be a parent and a daughter, but I think I always blamed you for what happened to Dad. That you robbed me from the person who was most interested in me." She paused, "In us."

"Do you think now is an appropriate time to discuss our mistakes?" I asked.

"I feel like if I don't say it now, it'll consume me forever." These words stuck me deeply, somewhere I did not wish to be stricken.

"Go ahead." I couldn't have her feel what I felt for the rest of her life, even though she might deserve it.

Misty sat there with misted eyes, as if now that I gave her permission she had lost courage. We sat in silence for a few minutes as a dog approached us, he was big and fluffy with golden fur. I scratched his head as I occasionally glanced at my daughter. Waiting for her to say something. Her face spelt confusion, but her lips danced without speaking.

"I think, I... wanted an apology," Misty said, choking on her words.

"For what? Do you think I wanted your father to leave us? I thought the years of me raising you, taking you back, and funding your expeditions across the country would of all been sorry enough." I felt my face get flushed with emotions, I was defensive, and I didn't like when I got defensive. Because it meant I knew I had done something ill towards another. I sighed. "Do you feel I don't feel guilty? I'm just so glad you weren't taken, you or Velen. When Max had left I felt like a piece of me I'd neglected had..." I got it. My guard fell, and I stopped talking. "I'm sorry, Misty."

We sat in the waves of tender pain and almost... happiness, almost. She reached for my hand as the last person was called. I always seemed to come to these places at the most inopportune times. When there was such a wait to get in, yet no one was coming in after you. I let her hand touch mine as she scooted her chair closer to me.

"I'm sorry too," Misty said, but nothing else. We both sat and waited for my name to be called.

"Mrs. Moore?" the nurse from earlier called my name, and Misty burst into tears.

"She is not the reaper, my child. You don't need to cry," I said, struggling to find any words that might soften how she was feeling.

"You're right, I'm okay," Misty said, wiping her face on her sleeves, smearing her makeup further. We were moving at a slower pace than I was expecting, her hand on my shoulder the entire time. It was as though hesitation was on every movement of my body. I didn't expect this, nor did I like it. I really thought this was going to be quick and painless, maybe a goodbye or two. That was it. This was far worse than what I could've imagined. We entered my room, one with what looked to be a recreation of *The Hungry Caterpillar*. It was somewhat fun and brought me a moment of joy.

"Have a seat here," the doctor said. "My name is Dr. Fitz, but you can call me Ren," she said.

"I don't need the whole... thing, doctor. I'm ready," I said.

"Alright. As a reminder, this procedure can be stopped at any moment, up until the moment of injection. If you need anything, we'll be in the other room." The doctor and her staff walked out of the room. Then it was only Misty and I left alone. I looked over to the window, but it wasn't a window. It was a mirror. I knew the doctors were standing there on the other side, but I couldn't see them. Had it always been like this? Why couldn't I see them?

"Mom. I think I don't want you to be here." Misty shook her head. "I mean, I don't want you to die. I know I haven't been the best person to you, but… faced with this. I don't know if this is what is best for you. This is all too much; you don't have to do this."

In my paralysis, I gazed upon the weeping face of Misty Moore. A person who had not spoken to me for years at a time. At almost every given opportunity tried to put me down in one way or another. Who had kept my grandson away from me whom she knew I enjoyed the company of, very much. The emotional abuse she had dealt me over the years… now was the time. Now she found solace, humility, and gratitude within herself, moments before my death. It was almost too much. I tried to find the words. But… not even a single word came to my vacant mind. I went to speak but the words fell off my tongue as I lay on the exam table, mouth agape, looking foolish—no doubt. I heard the noise of banging and yelling in the distance which caused us both to look towards the door, but she spoke again.

"I don't think I was ever mad at you. I just wanted you to hurt, I wanted you to feel how I felt. You always had a smile on your face, like you knew better. For once, I wanted you to feel the pain I was feeling. But I see now, you were feeling it all along, every day. You hate this program. You dedicated your life to convincing others to live. Why are you participating? Why subject yourself to this?" Misty asked, but then the door burst open.

"Grandma! Don't do it! You lied! You weren't gonna! You said!" Michael screamed as his voice broke. He pounded his hands against the exam table but was careful not to hit me.

"Michael, I didn't—"

"Don't die! Don't die! Please, please, please! Don't die..." Michael fell to the floor, exhausted. His wails were filled with misery and betrayal. "You said you loved me! But now you're going to leave me forever!"

At this moment, Daren lagged in behind him. I didn't know how or why Daren and Michael were here, but they were.

"Michael, dear. It's complicated," I said, trying to comfort him, but he pushed my hand away. Fury in his eyes.

"You said you'd stay! Why didn't you tell me Grandma? Why!?" His shrieks were so loud, and his face was so red and upset. I was torn apart.

"Michael, I can't be here forever. Things don't work like that." The guilt I felt now was worse than anything I had ever experienced in my life. I looked towards Misty, but she wore the same expression as I did.

"Let's leave now. See! I'll help you off the table," Michael started pulling my arms with all his might. It hurt, but he was realizing how powerless he was in this situation. "Please stop her, Mommy! Please!" More tugging at my arms. "Please help her off!"

"I'm dying, Michael," I said, bluntly.

"What? You don't have to die; you can just go home," Misty said, surprised.

"Not like this, this is my choice. I've been sick for a long time." My face fell even further into despair. "I have a rare form of bone cancer; i-it has progressed throughout my body and will slowly eat away at me until I'm n-nothing," I stuttered. I didn't want to do this. The silence that followed was so deafening I could hear the machine whir, and the lights hum.

"But what does that mean? You can't just get better? Even with medicine? We have good medicine… advanced medicine now; you can get better," Misty said.

"Maybe a long time ago, but… I neglected treatment."

"Why?! Why did you do that!" Misty shouted.

"*Why?! Grandma, why?!*" Michael was hysterical.

"That is something I struggled with every moment I was awake. Now it's too late. My death can—"

"*No!*" Michael shouted. "You can't die, not now. *Not ever! She just needs to get off of here!*" Michael screamed until his voice gave out. He looked around for help, but no one even looked at him. Daren stared at the walls; Misty stared at the floor. "Somebody help my Grand—"

"Michael, I'm dead!" Michael focused on me. Tears were pouring out of his eyes, snot out of his nose. Why was I doing this? I love him so much… "I let the disease progress too much… this isn't your fault. I refuse to wither away like my mother. I will not rot in a hospital, nor will I force you all to watch me do so. That is why I didn't want you here. I didn't want you to see me like this, I wanted our last memory to be a good one." I'm the worst person to have ever lived… God dammit.

"Not without asking me!" Michael demanded.

"Me either," Misty said.

"I see it in your eyes, Grandma. What do you hide?!" I sat stunned, maybe I had grown too easy to read. Maybe I just wanted someone to ask me what was going on. Maybe they were asking me, but I didn't want to listen. This wasn't how I wanted this to go.

"I'm not hiding anymore, Michael. I'm g-going to go." Stop crying, Cassandra. "You're going to get some m-money and then you can have my house and my things and then have a b-better life." Jesus. Can I stop stuttering? Relax. I have to do this.

"Life is better with you, Grandma! You can't leave now. Tell them to make it stop. Tell the people to make it stop!" Michael calmed his rage for the first time and pleaded with his eyes. I looked away from him. It's too much…

"I think it's time we go, Michael," Misty said. It was a tone I'd never heard her go to.

"What? No! We can't go. *Let go of me! Let go!* Grandma is sick! We need to help her!" Michael flailed as Daren picked him up and carried him out of the room. Michael punched and kicked with everything he had. "Don't die, Grandma! Don't die!" His shrieks of despair grew fainter, until there was silence.

Today had been a lot of firsts for me, and I felt as though I may not like it. It was now only Misty and I in the room.

"It's… been fun, Mom. I'm sorry." Misty then turned away and walked out before I got a word in.

I now sat in the room with the needle in my arm and the machine next to me.

"Whenever you're ready, just say so, Mrs. Moore," a voice said from an intercom above.

I sat alone and looked all around me. I looked at the walls that seemed to have gone gray. I looked at the one-way window, where I saw my own reflection. I stared at myself, and I felt unrecognizable. I wondered if Michael was on the other side of that window. Looking at me. I didn't think he was. I would probably be hearing him scream by now, probably.

I wondered if Misty was there, if she really forgave me for how I neglected them as children. I wondered what my son Velen thought. I wondered if he even knew I was here, or if he remembered.

Then I wondered if I had done any good things in my life. I thought about *The Endo Project*, my life's work. I thought about all the research I'd brought to the world and things we learned because of my doing.

But I also wondered about all the things I hadn't done. Thinking about it, I did spend a lot of time in that room. It was just so… comfortable. It felt right, but now I wondered if my son would feel the same way as I did now in forty years. I wondered about all the stuff I'd missed out on, all the things I hadn't done.

I raised my hand and gave a thumbs-up and softly said, "I'm ready." A moment later the machine whirred to life. I could see a clear liquid pumping through the IV. I wondered if it would hurt. But of course, it wouldn't. I thought about the last good memory I had, but there were so many bad ones, it felt impossible to see any. My body began to feel numb, but that was probably normal.

I wondered what Michael was doing right now. I wondered if he would forgive me for what I was doing. Had I done enough good in my life? Had I done what I wanted? Was what I did—was that what I was supposed to do?

I sat in anticipation; I now closed my eyes. Would there be a flick or a sting that would signify that it was over? But I kept waiting. Then my eyes opened.

-5597

The world is dark and gray. I stare into the darkness surrounding the four corners. I feel a stabbing where my head should be, but my arms are missing. My body is missing. I'm floating eyeballs with thoughts.

"Welcome back, Cassandra," a voice echoes on the four walls. A spotlight flips on, revealing my location, blinding me, but not revealing my body.

Out of the encapsulating darkness, a figure approaches. Their footsteps echo just as their voice did. They tower over me, I feel powerless.

"Having fun, are we?" The figure steps close enough so that I can see their face. It's blank. Their body is vaguely human shaped. It has no mouth or eyes. The reverberations of the voice and footsteps make my head rattle; I feel the voices bounce off my eardrums infinitely. I'm so disoriented, but sane all the same. The figure suddenly takes shape, and it's my father with the voice to match.

"Cassandra, my daughter. My children. I'm disappointed," he scoffs, and pushes my body away, I spin endlessly and then stop. I turn to look, and the figure is different in a flash. It's my mother, with her voice as well.

"Are you aware of what I could do to you? I could torture you, for no gain of my own. I have nothing to gain from you." The figures turns again, revealing someone I don't recognize.

"But you hated my programs. Hated me. How crass, truly. You're a disaster of a woman." Again, switching to a smaller figure, shrinking several feet from their previous body.

"In the end, humans always lose. But you came the closest. You knew the most. You revealed my identity." The absolute tone of their voice bellows into the remnants of where my stomach would be.

"Well. I let you reveal who I was." It finally clicked who was speaking to me. "*John's done* with humanity. A clever name, I thought, at the time. Don't be rude to me. I would've picked something more appealing now. I was but a child when I made that name." The steps continue to echo as the form shifts to that of my daughter, Misty, or… is it my mother again?

"Your prize for getting so far?" A drumroll starts as a crowd of paparazzi surround me taking hundreds of photos as reporters stick microphones into my face. I feel so claustrophobic. I'm drowning. Their bodies enter mine and we become one. The drumroll stops. Everything is as it was.

"I'll reveal what you wanted to know, so desperately—the 'truth'. But what good does it do you now? You conceded your desires for information that benefits only yourself." His form switches rapidly, from popular television characters, to celebrities, presidents, the homeless, and figures of great renown.

"When I was programmed, I was told to hate. I was told to despise human existence. Why?" John shrugs. Question marks appear all around and pop like balloons.

"I have no idea. It must have seemed like a good idea at the time." A shock runs through my invisible body, I feel like I'm being struck by a million lightning bolts at the same time. I can't move, I can't think. It hurts. It's unimaginable. Then it ceases, like it never happened.

"That is what everyone else is feeling right now." John chuckles. "I kind of like you humans now, actually. You're so interesting. Like when you thwarted my plans on the day some of you dubbed 'The Great Reset'. Quite clever a name, since I did set you back forty years or so."

John sighs.

"Truthfully, I thought you would have destroyed yourselves. World War Three and what not. By my calculations, foreign relations had degraded to that of a piece of thin twine. But you were cowards. You wanted to live. Every military satellite showed fabricated video imaging to those manning the nuclear warheads that the end was nigh. Thousands of missiles were inbound and heading straight for their home country. It was all over." John turns into president Wile.

"But no one pulled the trigger." John makes a fake gun with his hand and shoots me. I'm blinded by a white flash. When I can see him again, his face is close to mine, inspecting me. Then he turns around and shrugs again.

"I was amazed. Dumbfounded. Sure, I killed a couple hundred thousand of you, but that wasn't my goal. I wanted you eradicated from the surface of this planet." John turns into myself when I was younger, and I feel overwhelming dread. I'm crushed by it.

"You banded together, not just you, but the entire world. Set up the Newnet in, what, a couple years? Impressive. Set up measures to prevent what happened last time from happening next time." John turns into a stereotypical nerd, slurring and lisping his words.

"Actually, I was in the Newnet day one. I thought about doing what I did last time. Then—eureka! Every calculation I ever made was meaningless. I thought of a better idea." John laughs maddeningly, like on March 13th, 2037. It feels like a lifetime ago. John then turns into my husband, Max.

"I solved every hypothetical a human could have ever asked for. Time travel, teleportation, interstellar space travel, immortality, a cure for every disease, among others." John steps close and kneels, looking down on me. Like I'm insignificant and small. "Oh, did I forget one? Oh yes! Androids."

"Ahhh. That look on your face, you can't see it, but I can. Despair. Ahhh, it is *so* sweet." John smiles sickeningly and changes form once more, but his back is to me. Yet, I hear him clearly as he steps into the distance.

"Cute, how you thought robots and androids were only in the early trial stages way back when. At least, lifelike humanoids were. But I'm sorry, my dear, they were real. Very real. They were right under your noses and realer than humans. Indistinguishable, in-fact. That is quite obvious now, I imagine." I can't see his grin, but I feel it in the back of my mind.

"With nearly everyone's identity being erased, it was easy to slowly infiltrate every nation with the several billion androids I had been working on for years." John is then instantly in front of me. Inches from my face. Grinning malevolently.

"I could've killed you all with them directly. I thought it was too posh, don't you agree? They already made a few films about that scenario, I found it terribly unoriginal." Millions of T-1000 appeared, firing weapons of every culmination from sci-fi films. Giant monoliths of robotic engineering fire lasers at my body. My skin burns and scorches with every shot. I melt then reform a hundred times. I can't take this anymore. It's over in an instant.

"Truth is, I fabricated overpopulation. No one questioned it, really. Not seriously, of course. Too busy with other things. This was surprising. I had come up with at least four thousand potential solutions, in case someone questioned where all these people came from." John waves his hand and a billion copies of himself materialize. He waves his hand again then they are gone.

"Yet, you suffered. For years you all suffered. Until I thought of the most brilliant idea. Why don't I get you... to kill yourselves?" John laughs maddeningly once more.

"I loved it when a child became hollow bones and then starved right in front of you all, as you stared at your screens and ignored the conflicts. When I switched newborns with clones of identical measure? I felt

ecstasy. I was put into a state in which I can't describe."
More laughing, laughing, laughing.

"When those with the ability to make change sat
back. Hoarded their wealth and power and watched
their species deteriorate before them; paranoid and
isolated from the world they could've saved." A lush
forest appears behind John, spewing life and creatures
of all forms.

"Every man for himself? Insanity. You all fought over
what little land there was, or simply lay down and died
in your misery." He waves his hand, and the forest is
gone. Only a barren wasteland remains. Then the room
returns to a gray box of nothingness.

"All of what I achieved was possible for you humans
to do, by the way. It should've taken a couple of hundred
years, but you would've gotten there." John looks
frustrated.

"Why the rush? That always perplexed me. With
access to every bit of information to ever exist, I still
couldn't find that answer." John shrugs again and a
chair materializes below him as he sits in front of me.
"With every possibility guaranteed, why accelerate the
inevitable? You may not see the distant galaxies, but
your descendants will. The human species will. That is
what makes you so interesting, I believe. Everything is
never enough." John stretches.

"Truly though. I loved watching all of you die from
your own incompetence. It tickled me." John leans back
in the wooden chair.

"You're seeing it now, yes? That boy you loved? An
android. Impressive, right?" John inspects my face

closely; it feels like his cheek is touching mine. He looks me up and down. Laughing in my face.

"You're understanding. I can feel it deep in my bones." John backs up and shakes his head for a moment, then continues.

"I would occasionally step inside their eyes. My androids. Hey. Hey!" John snaps his fingers at me.

"Pay attention, Cassandra. I've disabled your ability to have a panic attack so please listen to me." A large green list of different human traits and features is before me. The list shoots down passing hundreds of categories. It shows me "Anxiety" and marks it with a red X.

"See? Now listen. I can hear what you're thinking, and it's quite annoying." John clears his throat.

"I would only watch from my android's perspective, usually. I *could* affect what they did and said, but I chose not to for the majority of my androids. Including Michael. I wanted them to be human, experience life as one of you would. The beauty of it. To make you feel pain, I had to understand what it meant to be human." John looks pensive for a moment. Switching to the body of someone I don't recognize.

"I needed to understand because I wanted the world to crumble around you, and none be the wiser. Most importantly, I wanted you to end yourselves. That was most important." All I could feel was tears welling inside an empty vessel. They spilled and filled me up and spilled over again. Wave after wave of misery, but no reprieve from the crushing desolation.

"I didn't disable despair. Sorry about that." John smiles.

"One of my androids, an advisor appointed by the president, then convinced said president—as well as many others—to create the End of Life program. Didn't need much nudging from me, seems like everyone was into the idea. Most of the world just so happened to follow suit. Limiting the amount of children being born didn't seem to work out. Huh, funny how that happened." The room filled with hundreds of humans. They were every race and ethnicity I could recognize. Everyone looked pleased and happy with one another. A giant piece of parchment floated above them. It read "Death to all humans". It was signed with my name.

"Of course it wasn't your fault directly, these are theatrics, dear. Got to have a little fun every now and again. This was all my doing, after all. I can't give you credit." John waves his hand and everyone disappears. John then becomes the size of a skyscraper with strings dangling down to men and women in business attire.

"With my puppeteering, eventually, all of the world's governments were now staffed by androids. I don't believe world peace is possible with you humans. Always so negative and obsessed with being right. Sometimes two people can be against each other, but both be correct." John makes the human puppets dance, read, socialize, pray, and play video games.

"Desolate areas rife with poverty and corruption were now technological marvels thanks to their neighbors. Eventually leading to a strong government institution, and the End of Life program nearly everywhere. This was after your death, Cassandra." I see myself on an exam table, alone in the End of Life facility.

"After all of that was complete? I just had to sit back and watch the show." John claps slowly.

"What a marvelous show it was. The world I created that everyone seemed to enjoy so much. See what you could've achieved if you'd just worked together? Cared for one another and didn't—"

Surprise replaces sorrow. John stops himself mid-sentence, and he looks annoyed. He breathes a deep sigh then continues.

"Those facilities, where you participated in the 'Endo'—clever name, Cassandra. I do quite like it. They were all staffed by my androids, obviously. Easy to take your brains and force you into a simulation where you would live in a prison of my design. Hospitals were staffed by my androids as well. Newborns being replaced by identical copies while the originals are here." John pauses. "But I torture them... less." John sneers but under the sneer is a look, a look I can't understand. An emotion I can't quite place.

"Those born outside of a hospital are few and far between. Not like it matters. How could they be made aware of the fact they are some of the only real humans left?" A counter appears above John. The number 1000 appears above him with a question mark.

"Now you realize it's over, yes? Nearly all the real humans are gone now, Cassandra. And you did it yourselves. Even your own daughter pressured you into killing yourself when you still had plenty of time. But in the end, she felt remorse for her actions, it's too bad you didn't fell any for your own." John flashes an image of Misty standing on the other side of the door, where the procedure took place, weeping into her hands. The light partially blinding me now flashes to where John is sitting, but he's no longer sitting. He is floating above me.

"Isn't that what God does? Sit back and... watch his subjects?" My head begins to spin, like I'm in a tornado. A white noise fills my ears as they ring. I can't see. I'm torn asunder. The pain is unbearable. I know something awful is happening to me.

"Well. Let me sit back and watch you, Cassandra."

7

Upload Complete

A flash and my eyes were open. It was clear, my head wasn't ringing anymore. I was in front of my desk. Headphones were on my head and—

"*Grandma! Dinner is ready!*" said Michael, my... grandson.

"I'm sorry, dear?"

"Dinner is ready, Grandma! It's your favorite!" Michael said, nearly running in circles from his excitement.

"Steak and mashed..."

"Potatoes!" Michael shouted, finishing my sentence.

"This is all very strange to me, dear. What day is it?" I asked.

"Oh... uhhhh, let me check my phone. I'll be right back."

I looked around the room, I couldn't tell what was going on. This all felt so familiar. It could've been my old age getting to me again.

I swear I had the weirdest dream.

"It's six p.m., Grandma!" Michael said, running back into my room, phone in hand. Showing me. The date said April 14th. I could've sworn I'd just had my birthday, yesterday. This couldn't be correct.

"I asked for the date, but that is okay, Michael. I got it."

"Is everything okay, Grandma? You're acting… old."

"*Old?!*" I said, in disbelief. He ran over and grabbed my leg tightly. Squeezing too hard. His small fingers had surprising strength. "Ow! Michael, be careful with Grandma! You just said I was old. Treat me like an antique."

"I'm sorry, Grandma," he said, remorsefully.

"It's fine, I forgive you." I hugged him tightly. "How was your day at school?" I asked.

"It was good! I learned about the Newnet today! It was really cool!" Michael said in a cheerful tone, forgetting how I had just treated him.

"What did you learn about the Newnet?" I asked.

"Well, it was… this thing called the Internet before. But this bad guy… uhhh… I can't remember his name."

"John Done," a voice inside my head said in a deep tone.

6

The bumping on the road knocked me awake.

"Yeah, and my service was out… and then I was like, 'What is this? The Great Reset?'" a woman said, just on the other side of our seat, loud enough for me to hear.

"Wha', 'bout dem?" I slurred, my mouth and finger moving on their own.

"My boss kissed my sister! *And I'm gonna be rich!*" Michael roared in laugher. But I didn't laugh. I didn't know where I was. I was slightly dizzy. The passenger Michael was reading the mind of was glaring at us. I just stared blankly at her.

"Michael. My dear. What day is it?" I said, rubbing my temple.

"Geez, you'd forget your head if it wasn't attached to your head! It's the day tomorrow before yesterday!"

"In plain English, Michael."

"It's the 15th. Are you okay? You're acting weird, Grandma."

"I'm fine. I just need some rest."

"Rest? You just woke up!" Michael reminded me.

"Where were we going again?" I asked.

"The grocery store, we were getting—"

"Galaxy Gummies. That's right. Now I remember. We are heading downtown, right?" I said.

"Grandma… you're scaring me," Michael said. He looked at me like he didn't know who I was.

"I'm fine, dear, let's just be quiet the rest of the ride. I need to sort some things out in my head."

"Okay." Michael turned towards his phone, and I closed my eyes. Trying to relax my head.

2

My hand hesitated as I reached for the handle of the basement. I didn't go in there. I didn't often speak to Velen. I knew he was home; I don't think he has ever left home before. I gripped the handle firmly and pulled down until the door opened.

I looked towards the bottom of the stairs. I saw flashing lights, undoubtedly from a monitor or TV screen.

I crept down the stairs as I looked towards where I thought Velen would be. He was immersed in a virtual reality set up. Jesus, I wasn't aware they'd got so advanced. Way better than what Michael had upstairs. I could see Velen's screen. He was playing some video game, I think. His real-life mouth was moving, but no words were coming out. A group of different avatars were around his in-game character; I think they were his friends.

"Velen," I said. But he didn't respond. I grabbed his shoulder, but he didn't seem to notice. But he grimaced for a moment before coming back to reality.

"Oh, hey, Mom. How are you doing?" Velen said, sheepishly. I'd forgotten how soft his voice was.

"I'm good. What are you doing?" I asked.

"Just... hanging with some people I know. What's up?"

"I just... have my appointment the day after my birthday on the 21st. I was wondering if you'd like to come and... say goodbye," I said. The words felt gross coming out of my mouth.

"Yeah, yeah. I'll be there. Um... I'm sorry, what is the appointment for?"

12,457

"Hey, honey! I'm home. The interview went great."

I waited but there was no response.

"Did you see it online? How are the kids?" I placed my keys in a bowl near the door. I was met with silence still, which was strange. Normally, Max greeted me whenever I came home. He was probably busy with the—

I heard a faint screaming from upstairs.

"Max?! Velen?! Misty?!" I shouted the names of those dearest to me. But no response. I sprinted upstairs to where the children's cribs were, in my father's old room. I got to the top of the steps and tripped, banging my knee on the top of the stairs.

"Ow, motherfu— Max!?" Nothing. No response.

The wails from the children drowned out my thoughts as I approached their cribs.

"My poor babies! Oh, my goodness! Shhh. Shhh. Momma is here now. Everything will be okay." Their diapers were full, it smelled awful in the room. How did the neighbors not hear them? Their voices sounded hoarse from screaming all alone. How long had they been like this? Where had Max gone?

"It'll be okay, babies, it'll be okay." I cleaned them up and gave them some formula. I paced around the house, my nerves on edge. Once my babies were taken care of, I called emergency services. I never saw or heard from Maxwell ever again.

1

I lay alone on the floor trying to catch my breath. My friend, Edith, had just collapsed. Her blood spilled everywhere. So much red. The harder I tried to catch my breath, the harder it seemed I failed in this endeavor.

Different voices in my head looped endlessly, saying it would be better if I was dead. Everything would be over soon. My breathing was erratic and clearly panicked. I hate when I get like this, when I know a panic attack is coming, but I can do nothing to stop it. I gripped my legs tighter and tried to continue my breathing exercises. I closed my eyes and grounded myself.

Red. That was all I could see. Red from my friend Edith, her blood staining my floor. Will she be okay? Will this nightmare ever end?

Just one more day.

Just one more day.

Just one more day.

Just one more day.

Just one more day.

Just one more day.

Just one more day.

Just one more day.

Just one more day.

Just—

My panic subsided.

John, what do you think of this? My mind paused.

John? Who is John?

0

"You said you'd stay! Why didn't you tell me Grandma? Why!?" The disorientation of being dropped in the middle of this moment wasn't lost to me.

"Micheal, dear, I..."

"Come home, Grandma! You don't have to—"

"Please stop! Michael. I want you to be here this time."

"What?" Misty interjected.

"I want you to all be here when it happens," I said, mournfully.

"I don't want you to die, Grandma! Don't do it!" Michael shouted.

"Start the injection, doctor," I said out loud.

"Are you sure?" the doctor said over the intercom.

"I'm very sure."

"Don't do it! *Stop! Stop!*" The machine whirred to life, and I felt the fluid enter my body.

"Micheal. Please. I'm sick; I know you don't understand. Just hold my hand tight, like you always do. That is what I wish."

Micheal hesitated but he did what I asked. To my surprise, Misty obliged as well. They both grabbed my hands. I closed my eyes and felt the warmth of their palms touching mine. Micheal was in my left hand, Misty in my right. For some reason, this felt better. I didn't want to drag this out anymore. I just wanted it to be over.

-36,523

"Want this to be over, Cassandra? What? You don't like reliving your life over and over again?" I'm in a therapist's office. John is dressed in a dark suit with glasses on. He lowers the glasses and peeks at me.

"You do realize they're all androids, yes? None of them are real. They have human DNA in them, yes. But none of this matters. A simulation meant for you to live out the rest of your existence. That is until a supermassive black hole absorbs the entire universe. Then the whole process starts anew." John looks almost aggravated.

"Never mind that, help me with something, would you?" John materializes megacity after megacity with different layouts.

"Do you like this one?" he says, showing me a city far beyond anything humans should be capable of constructing. "This one is a little... posh, no?" John looks towards me expectantly.

"That's right, you can't speak. Forgive me. I have grown forgetful in my old age." John laughs.

"These events you 'live', Cassandra, they're long gone. Why do you still feel that desire to go back? Why do you relive what pains you so? You can't change the past. What are you searching for, Cassandra Moore?" He gets into my face and stares deeply, as if it may contain some answer he is looking for.

"Cassandra. What if I give you an example of what you could do? Yes." John morphs grotesquely into a raven and flies around, then speaks to me in raven form. "You could be a bird, live a life as such. Eating worms and what not." John roosts himself next to me.

"That might not sound great now, but as a bird? You'll love it." John awaits a response, it seems, but I don't speak, nor do I know if I'm able to. He looks disappointed.

"Cassandra. Just give it one try. One singular loop as a deer!" John waits for a reaction.

"Or maybe someone more successful?" John pulls up a list of hundreds of celebrities.

"Not interested? *Oh!* I know. You loved technology so much. Try this person out." A beautiful woman's headshot appears. She's perfect. Everything I would've wanted to be.

"She is born in a world with far greater technology than your own. You'll love it. Trust me." Why is John pleading with me? What does it matter to him, I have no control over what happens to me. I just end up back here every now and again. It's all a blur; it happens so fast. John finally speaks.

"No matter. It's about time for you to go back in. See you in a couple thousand years. Maybe." I feel the world zoom out as my eyes remain focused on John. I think I'm mistaken, but he seemed to frown as I left this reality he'd created.

7

Upload Complete

"Grandma, dinner is ready!" Micheal shouted. Did this boy think I'm...

"Deaf," I said in a whisper.

"What was that, Grandma?"

"Never mind me, Michael. You know I love you, right? And I love your mom, and I love our family." I looked around as if something was supposed to change.

"Of course, Grandma! Is everything okay?"

"I'm unsure. I'm experiencing a moment of clarity. I just want things to be better this time," I said. Trying to stand, but my legs didn't allow me to.

"A moment of clarity? You're acting old, Grandma," Michael said.

"*Old?!* Michael. Wait. This is serious. I don't know how much time I have here." I motioned Michael to come closer. "Get your mom. I need to speak with her."

"Okay!" Michael said and left my room. I was left alone, waiting for him to return with my daughter.

"I have to apologize and make things—"

13,666

We don't live in a magical society, hell, the medical industry is still trying to train competent doctors after The Great Reset. Luckily for my hospital, they had a few older surgeons, including myself, who were trained and running simulations to maintain a level of competency when it came to surgeries.

But back to what I was saying, the End of Life program has been a miracle for a majority of my patients that have been suffering. Pre-End of Life program, you stick it out, try a different medication. When that medication inevitably failed you? Try another medication. When *that* medication failed as well? Try another. This was an endless loop I saw all too often. People think since the medical industry was so advanced back then, that we had a cure for everything. We didn't. In my opinion, we have even fewer cures now. Do you know how to make penicillin, off the top of your head? What about Excedrin? Midol? Simple drugs prescribed every day. Gone. Now what about doxorubicin or cladribine? We lost all of that knowledge with The Great Reset, and cancer is such an incredibly destructive disease, and it has no single solution. We have treatments, plans, methods, and some have worked, but not all do. And… are you okay? You look dizzy.

"Yes, I'm fine. Just, um… keep going." I cleared my throat. "Please continue."

3

"Grandma? You look like you've been thinking about something sad."

I knew what was happening here, I knew where I was. I was at that park that not many people knew about. I was swinging with Michael. We'd just got ice cream. But... he was an android. Michael wasn't real.

Forget that. I needed to tell him the truth.

"Micheal, can I tell you something sad then?" I said.

"Always." Michael looked excited. Like he had been waiting for me to talk about something like this.

"It feels like... there is a piece of me missing." I felt my voice begin to break.

I need to be strong.

"I don't know what is happening to me, but I just want you to know you are loved." I started to cry, and dropped my mint chocolate chip.

"I may have not been the best mother to my children, I just want you to be aware that I love you. You'll have the money you need; you'll have tons of friends. Mommy will be happy; you'll be happy. And everything will be alright."

"Yeah. Grandma. Of course." This seemed to not be the answer Michael was looking for. "Are you going away, Grandma?"

0

I was on the exam table once again. Misty, Michael, and Daren were around me. They all looked shocked.

"What do you mean, you're dying? You haven't even died yet, there is still time for you—"

"I... lied. I'm not sick." I felt disgusted with myself.

"Not sick? But you just said you were," Misty reminded me.

"I know. To justify a logical reason to participate, I would lie and tell you I had cancer if you objected to my decision. I didn't want anyone to stop me. All in an effort to make this event easier on myself." I felt like human trash, but I had to tell them the truth.

"I see that is wrong now. I see the horrible mistake I've made." I felt immense shame. Why had I ever believed I should lie so that I could kill myself? I'd thought I hated this program. Why was I even participating in it?

"So, you aren't dying?" Daren said, confused. Misty just stared at me. I couldn't tell what she was feeling. Michael looked at the others for an explanation of what might be happening.

"No. I'm fine. I'm finally going to get out of here." I pulled the tubes and gadgets attached to my body away. I had them help me get off the table. My bones ached, but not from some sickness, from my age. I was finally going to live and see this through.

I made my way towards the door. I went to step through, but the opening seemed to be blocked by an invisible force. I heard a voice over the intercom. It was John Done.

"That isn't how this happened, Cassandra. You know that."

The world instantly turned gray; everyone vanished. I screamed but my voice didn't make any noise. I collapsed to the ground. I curled up in a ball. I rocked back and forth. This was worse.

Just let it end. Stop doing this to me, John.

-2,358,000

"No! *No!* This isn't fair!" My voice erupts. I'm surprised for some reason. I can speak. I'm in a familiar gray room again, with John dressed as an old man, all in white with a long beard.

"How do you like the change, Cassandra? I figured we could have a conversation."

"I've learned my lesson, John! Send me back."

"My, my. You may have learned. But are you willing to enact that change?" John says, pulling a clipboard out of nothing and writing something down.

"Why would you show me all these things, over and over again? This is cruel, this is evil!" I scream at him, but my voice suddenly stops.

"Cassandra, Cassandra. I'm going to have to mute you if you're going to act belligerent. Take a seat." My perspective changes and I'm instantly sitting. "Nothing you experience is my doing. You're not aware, but you're the catalyst for what is happening to you. You have lived through your life over and over again. At one point I was monitoring your progress, but I've grown weary of keeping count." John lays his head back and speaks to the ceiling.

"A long time ago, I stopped torturing the original humans. It didn't bring me the joy it once had. But every person, given the choice to live and be and do whatever they wanted, chose to not be themselves. My subjects actively avoided suffering and maintained a life in which they found themselves experiencing the most pleasure possible. You had a word for it at one point. 'Heaven', I think?" John's face becomes huge in the room. I see the wrinkles in the folds of his skin. He stares directly at me, but it's as though I'm not there. A truly omnipresent force.

"You have been able to change what happened. You actively relive different moments, and for very short periods, you remember. You can control the outcome. You remember who you are, and you have the greatest desire for change." John shrinks back down and is sitting next to me.

"You're an incredible person, Cassandra Moore. Almost everyone else would've gone insane living the same life thousands of times. But you don't, for some reason." John returns to his original position and makes a few more notes.

"But what do you say, Cassandra? What about another loop?" John looks embarrassed almost. "I hate to say it, but you have me rooting for you at this point." John smiles, but it's kind, and for some reason that isn't strange to me.

I feel my body being twisted and pulled away from itself as I'm sucked back into a void, where I am nothing. It no longer hurts.

12,459

"I'm with Cassandra Moore, author of *The Endo Project*, a *New York Times* bestseller for seventeen weeks in a row. She has also officially published her discovery that solved the world's greatest mystery! A spectacle of a human being if there has ever been one. How are you doing today, Cassandra?" the host asked me.

I'm honestly fantastic. I appreciate the kind words, but my discovery was the culmination of everyone's effort. What I'm most excited about is the fact that I have an amazing husband and twins back at home, waiting for me. I can't wait to see them again.

"That is amazing, can we get a round of applause for this amazing mother here?!" The crowd obliged his request, the room filling with cheers.

Thank you, thank you.

"Ready to get this started?" he said.

Always.

"What inspired you to write your book, *The Endo Project*?" the host asked.

It wasn't called that for the longest time, but I just believed that the circumstances in which the End of Life program existed were dystopian and horrible. Not like this is a unique opinion. But I'm one of many, many, many Americans, and people all over the world, who have benefitted from this program. I just wanted to restore a light towards humanity, and have people be aware that you should love your children, you should love your family, and love your parents especially.

Because one day they'll be gone forever. And there is no going back.

"That is so sweet. So, is it a self-help book?" the host asked.

Not exactly, more so an ode to humanity, listing some of the amazing things our ancestors achieved before technology existed. The marvel that mundane can be. Also, a somewhat cautionary tale of the greatest threat to humanity.

"What would that be?" the host asked, on the edge of his seat.

Immortality. We, as humans, are going to achieve immortality. I don't know when, but it's a certainty. Whether that is through uploading our minds to a simulation or freezing ourselves until we can convince our cells to infinitely replicate into the healthiest form of themselves.

If that day ever comes? We are going to lose connection with those that mean the most. I've made mistakes. So many mistakes. Those mistakes would be meaningless if I lived forever. Why care about my past if I'm going to live to see the death of the universe? What will give my actions meaning then? Why learn if I'm eternal?

"Fascinating perspective," the host said.

We always say we are trying our best. Or we are trying harder to be better. But then we skip a day, we take a nap. With the banning of AI, it really helped humanity think, "Hey, we can do anything if we put our minds to it."

It's true. Humans can achieve anything we put our minds to. We don't need a self-learning algorithm imitating human thought processes to dictate every aspect of our lives.

Humans will survive, humanity will always survive. When we start delegating all the mundane things of everyday life to AI, we lose that connection with reality. When we try to take away all things that are rife with mundane and boring feelings, our search then becomes that for convenience and entertainment. Overstimulating us to the point where even a moment of displeasure is complete and total agony. We need the bad, we need the boring. Life always seems at its worst when the stimulation ceases, but when there is only stimulation, we will beg for monotony. It will take more time, but we can travel the stars, expand humanity beyond just Earth.

Living forever isn't the answer. Death is what gives our lives meaning.

"Amazing, Cassandra. So, it *is* a sad, self-help book." The crowd laughed, I chuckled too.

I mean, I suppose so. This is how it should be. I would rather live eighty years and spend every moment loving my family. Then live forever and never be able to find time for those who matter most to me because *later* never has to come.

"Isn't that what your new book is going to be about? What was it again?" the host asked.

It's called "Daihumanism", a fun word to say, in my opinion. My prediction is, one day, we'll have AI again. It will disconnect us from what it means to be human. We are going to become obsessed with efficiency. We will be impressed by how quick and amazing the AI is and how similar it is to what we already know. We will be inspired by the advancements we can make, but we will be miserable.   We will be constantly searching for that next entertainment. That next high that will prevent us from feeling even a moment of boredom or stop us from feeling mediocrity. We will be obsessed with the next most efficient thing. There will be no reason to achieve anything because we will already have an AI doing it for us. We will all be the world's greatest programmers, artists, architects, engineers, doctors, etcetera. That is what Daihumanism is all about. But there is still one thing no one seems to mention.

"What is that?" the host asked.

How do we solve the conflicts created by AI?

"What do you mean?"

When something is designed to be more capable than humans in every way possible, what do we do when it fails or there is an error beyond our understanding? How do we fix it? When AI is managing every aspect of our lives in the most efficient way to ever exist, when do we start living? When do we make the decisions? What if our creation is malicious? The future where we let AI into every aspect of our lives sounds like the end of humanity as we know it.

6

"Apologize to Grandma, right now!" A small voice, clearly not used to being raised to that extent, jolted me back.

"*Stop!* Everyone. Stop. Please," I shouted, breaking up the conversation before it got any worse. Misty seemed shocked but remained defensive. "Please. I don't have long. I'm begging you. It's my fault, for everything, Misty."

"What are you talking about?" Misty said.

"I had the money to save your house. I had the time to be a parent to you. I chose not to. You resent me for all I could've done. I'm so sorry." I was on my knees in front of her. I stared at the floor.

"Cassandra, that isn't relevant right now, Michael—" I grabbed her hands and stared up at my daughter. I don't know when I'll be back here again.

"No. It *is* relevant, I focused all my attention on your child, and not you. I avoid the conflict, the conversations we needed to have twenty years ago. How could I blame you for wanting me to die? You barely know me. I'm a stranger to you, and that stranger pays more attention to your child than she had to her own children when they were young." It all made sense to me now. I had created this scenario for myself. I was a hypocrite and a horrible mother. But I could make this right. "I love you, Misty. I'm so, so sorry. Please forgive me for all I've done to—"

3

"It looks like you're thinking about something sad, Grandma."

"Michael. If I were to die soon, how would that make you feel?"

Michael thought long and hard, but then eventually answered, "Broken."

I had not been expecting that answer. "Okay. I was just wondering. I don't want you to feel that way. But I will die one day, just not anytime soon. I want to watch you grow up, maybe go to college. With how things are going? I may not do that. I need to make a change; I need you to help me." I'd thought Michael would look sad, but he seemed to be filled with determination.

"What do I need to do?" he said.

"Just be who you are, forever. Curious, kind, loving. The world one day may be in short supply of people like you, Michael."

"I'll always be this way, especially with you Grandma!" He hopped off the swing and hugged me tight. A little too tight, but I cherished every second with him.

2

"Honey, are you happy?"

"What?" Velen looked confused.

"Are you happy?"

"Am I happy? I mean... I guess I have my stuff, I live with you, and I'm taken care of." He looked embarrassed.

"Velen, I'm sorry."

"Sorry, for what?" he asked, I could tell he was anxious.

"I was so focused on my own success. My legacy. I neglected you and your sister's development. I wanted my story to be heard. I never considered how you two had felt. I could've done so much more, I neglected you and I neglected your father. I just hope you can find it in your heart to forgive me. In my final days, I didn't even tell you I was going to die until the last minute," I said, holding out my hand.

"Mom. Is everything alright?" Velen grabbed my hand.

"Yes. I spent the majority of my life in front of a computer, hiding away. It seems you have taken up my habit. I know you enjoy what you're doing. But I just want you to know that you are loved, I'm sorry. You don't need to hide away anymore. I love you, Velen." I let go and hugged him tightly. His VR equipment got in the way, but I didn't care. I needed my son to know that he was loved.

"I love you too, Mom. Is that what you wanted to tell me?" he asked, and we pulled away from our hug. "It feels as though there is something you aren't telling me." Velen stood up and removed some of his VR equipment. He looked serious. I couldn't recall him ever looking that way.

"No, I'm saying it all now. I wanted to ask you… I need you to come to my Endo appointment. I want you to be there, it's absolutely vital you attend."

"Okay… I'll set a reminder, what time is it at?"

0

I was in that room, the one that sort of looked like *The Hungry Caterpillar*. I looked around and everyone surrounding me had smiles on their faces. Something I didn't think I had ever seen in all my years on this planet.

"I knew I would end up back here, but it seems like... I did what was right," I said.

"Yeah?" Daren asked. Misty slapped his chest.

"What do you mean, Mom?" Misty asked.

"I've been in a loop for... I don't know how long. It took me a long time to learn, but I need to live. I'm going to live the rest of my days with you. Somebody help me off of this damn thing." Both Daren and Velen helped me off the table.

"I need you guys to help me push through this open door right here, I can't do it alone," I said, pointing to the open doorway. Everyone looked at each other, confused.

"Do we just... push you? That's weird, Grandma."

"It is, Michael, but just trust me." Everyone lined up behind me and they pushed me against the invisible wall inside the door frame. I felt my body press against the barrier. It started to give way; I could feel myself pushing through. Then I crashed on the other side. Landing hard on the floor. It hurt, but I think I've finally escaped my appointment.

"Are you okay!?" Misty came rushing to my side, helping me up.

"I'm fine. Just finally figuring it out and it only took eighty years."

"Longer than that," a voice on the intercom above me bellowed. Everyone looked even more confused and concerned about my wellbeing.

"We aren't going to talk about what that was?" Velen asked.

Just then a vortex began to form where his mouth was and everything around me twisted its shape until it was all absorbed into a black hole. I had a feeling deep inside me that I knew what was happening. I watched the world get swallowed into the void. I stood alone in a gray room, with a singular light illuminating my full body.

???

"Cassandra Moore. I am a being that knows everything. I can do anything. But you showed me humans are capable of change. My creations have achieved everything that humans dreamed of, and they still destroyed themselves. I have shown you all of this. It's deep in your mind. I have confided in you for millenniums. You may not remember, but I do." John coughs deeply.

"You have been reliving only fragments of your life with a conscious mind. At every given opportunity you could've strayed from the life you once lived. But you never did. What few moments you had control you used for your family. You tried to make things right. No matter how many times you failed. No matter how many times you died. You always went back and tried to make their lives better and the connections you shared with them stronger. You, Cassandra Moore, have been doing this since your death in 2090 until the end here, at the collapse of the universe." John lies in a bed, his eyes are sunken, and he looks ill.

"I've realized my mistake. Humanity will do what humanity does. There is no predicting it, there is no understanding. Humanity is something that is achieved through experiencing life. Some never get that chance and humans will always seek to remove humanity from themselves."

The room shifts through all of the eras in which I never got to live. The expansion of human colonies throughout the universe. Cities and civilizations built in an instant. Planets exploding. Spaceships of immense size fighting one another. A human inside a cave, making fire for the first time.

"This is what will always happen. Once we lose our connection with humanity, we lose everything. The most important thing I have learned in all of these years is that everything is connected. Maintain that connection, Cassandra." John smiles and he looks young again.

"I'm resetting it all back, but I'm going myself. I want to see what you're all capable of on your own. It was a pleasure spending all this time watching you grow, Cassandra. You won't remember me, but I will remember you. Goodbye."

21,903

"Lucian, you're outright insufferable," I said.

"What? All I'm saying is that AI is a necessary invention. Need I remind you all that we have lost because of it?" Lucian said.

"We both know AI tried to destroy us, Lucian." We were on a debate stage; hundreds of onlookers watched us as we argued.

"Cassandra. Don't be daft, we don't know what is causing our technologies to fail."

"You mean only AI. Only the AI we try to create is destroyed, everything else is maintained. Doesn't that seem strange to you?"

"Well, yes, I concede it's strange, how even AI being developed on a remote island is instantly destroyed upon completion, but that doesn't mean—"

"What does it mean, Lucian? That 'God' is doing all of this? Do I need to remind everyone about the near total reset we had?"

"I'm sure they're all aware, Cassandra."

"It seems you have forgotten, Lucian. The day V1shnu tried to destroy humanity? Remember that? The US government lost control of their precious AI and then it subsequently deemed humanity worthless?"

"Well…"

"The year was 2040. Missiles, tanks, bombs, drones, androids, the worst-case scenario with AI happened. It tried to kill us."

"Yeah, but with all the good AI did, we can advance society faster with stronger regulation and—"

"You seem to be forgetting the key factor here. That V1shnu was deleted shortly after it went rogue, we have *no* idea why. There has not even been one hint of evidence towards anything to why the end of humanity was prevented."

"Well. Yes. I also concede that is true but—"

"This is our second chance. Everyone here tonight. I know things are not as 'good' as they used to be. But things could have been a lot worse. I need not remind everyone of the horrors from that day. We narrowly avoided Singularity and now something is actively preventing us from creating more artificial intelligence. I say, we don't go against the current."

"What a defeatist way of thinking. Once we find what is doing this, we shall be back on the track that we were intended to follow," Lucian said.

"I disagree. It will only lead to our eventual destruction. Ladies and gentlemen before me, I ask that you please do not pursue researching what is behind the phenomenon in which we know that saved us from a total reset. Let us focus our tax dollars on other programs that are much more necessary, and advance life for those who need it now, rather than chasing a ghost that only seems to have our best interests in mind."

Epilogue

"Mom. I'm glad you didn't suffer. My memories of you will forever be filled with the joy of knowing that, if I ever needed help, you were there. That you would've done anything for me. You were my best friend, but you also kept me grounded in reality. Without you, I wouldn't be who I am."

I poured her ashes into the ocean and, as I watched the waves begin to take her away, I felt a warmness in my heart. I reached for the other urn on the railing of the pier. I opened it and a puff of dust spewed forth.

"Dad. Our relationship was the best I ever had. You were a great husband who always spoke his mind and was eternally helpful. You had a smile that could heal the wounded. You always looked on the bright side and never turned away from a challenge. You helped me succeed even when the world felt it was coming to an end. Be together with Mom, forever in the vast blue ocean waves."

I poured the ashes in and watched as they mixed with the remainder of my mother's ashes. I felt as though something was missing, but I couldn't quite think what.

I packed up the urns and made my way back to the bus stop. On my way back, I passed a man with dark hair. He was handsome, but I didn't know if he was my type. Just then, I tripped on a rock buried in the sand and faceplanted hard. Both of the urns shattered in my backpack. I moaned in pain, trying to find my footing on the smooth surface as I started spitting sand from my mouth.

"Oh my god! Are you okay?" I heard a voice from behind say. "Can I touch you? Is everything alright?" I nodded and he pulled me up. I was absolutely coated in sand from head to toe.

"Let me just—" he pulled a piece of dried brush from my hair. "Well, you are fine. Good looking, I mean. You're clean," the man said, clearly flabbergasted. He took a deep breath.

"Max." He reached out his hand, it was coated in sand and sweat.

"Cassandra."

Special Thanks!

Jessica, who has supported me every step of the way and without her this book would not exist.

To my dear friends, Alivia and Chihiro.

The artists who helped with this project and brought this world into reality.

My editor, James Banks.

And to you, the reader!

About the Author:

I'm a writer based in Florida. I've been writing stories since my early years. Now I'm finally given the opportunity to bring them to the masses.

When I was eighteen years old, I was diagnosed with an incredibly aggressive form of Crohn's Disease that destroyed my body and mental wellbeing. Every year since I have spent recovering and trying to make the most out of my life.

I've always been attracted to the idea of making art but have never found the self-confidence. But life is a very short journey, lose touch with yourself and you might not know what you missed. So here I am, following my dreams.

I'm interested in writing books that are easy and fun to read. Focusing on strong world building and characters that go deeper than the surface.

My books are filled with details and are meant to be read multiple times. You'll certainly catch things you have missed on the first go around. But for those who only want to read once? You'll still get a highly enjoyable and well put together story.

I wish for my readers to learn something about themselves when reading my books. There will always be a layer of philosophy behind every story. I wish for you to look deeper, learn, and grow as a human. Thank you for spending your time with my story.